EXTra ROOMS

R. MERRILL

D1319518

New Creation Publishing

But he [Stephen], being full of the Holy Spirit, looked up sted-
fastly into heaven, and saw the glory of God, and Jesus standing
on the right hand of God, and said, Behold, I see the heavens
opened, and the Son of Man standing on the right hand of God.

–Acts 7:55-56

CHAPTER 1

Stephen sat in his rented sedan and stared at the old house up the street. Freshly cut lawn, neatly trimmed hedges, flowers blooming along the clean-swept walkway. Someone strolling by would never guess that the only person who lived there was on her death bed. The house looked so loved. Cared for. Not a speck of peeling paint in sight.

Stephen didn't want to get out of the car. He didn't want to be here at all. Not in Maine. Not in the tiny town of Jay. Certainly not on this street. There were way too many people here. People he hadn't seen in years. People he hadn't missed.

No one had warned him that these people would be here, though now that he thought about it, of course they would be. He wasn't the only one running out of time to say goodbye.

Knuckles rapped on his window, making him jump, and he looked out to see his least favorite cousin smiling down on him like they were old pals.

Stephen rolled his window down. "Hey, Patrick."

"Hey, Stevieboy!"

Stephen tried not to grimace.

"You just gonna sit here or what? And what's with the Massachusetts plates? I thought you lived in Texas!"

And the hits just keep coming.

Patrick leaned on the door and stuck his head into the car like he was going to give Stephen a big smooch.

Stephen veered right. "Hang on a sec." He started to roll the window up, and Patrick pulled his head back like a spooked dog. Then he jumped back when Stephen opened the door.

"It's Tennessee, and this is a rental." He slammed his door shut and started toward the house.

Patrick fell into step behind him. "Did you just get here?"

"Yes," Stephen said.

"Nana said you were staying for a few days?"

"Maybe." Nana had asked him to spend the night, but he was going to try to get out of it. At fourteen, he'd vowed to never again spend the night here. He didn't plan to break that vow at the age of twenty-eight.

"Carrie and Jeremiah are staying here, but I've got to work, so I'm bouncing back and forth." He uttered a guttural chuckle. "It's been kind of nice, having my house to myself."

How nice for him. His grandmother was dying, his wife was tending to her, and he was enjoying his break from his family.

"Nana wants a little kid running around while she's in hospice?" Stephen didn't try to disguise his snark.

"Oh, Jeremiah is so quiet that people don't even know he's there." He laughed. "Cripes, he's so quiet he's a little creepy ... Hey, that's what we used to say about you." He punched him in the shoulder, and Stephen glared at him. "But for real, Nana adores him. She likes having him around no matter how bad she feels."

Thankful to have reached the house, Stephen trotted up the steps to get ahead of and away from Patrick, but then when he got to the door, he froze. His fourteen-year-old self was still inside him, begging him not to go any further.

It's okay, he told himself, *you're not going to sleep here.*

He reached for the door and, feeling Patrick's judgment from behind, pushed it open and stepped inside.

Nothing weird happened, and he knew he'd been foolish to think that it might. It was just a house, and he was wide awake.

His mother caught his eye and strode across the living room toward him. "Stephen!" She wrapped her arms around him and squeezed tight. "When did you get in, honey?"

"About two o'clock."

She stepped back and rubbed his arm. "I told you I would pick you up at the airport."

"No, no. It's easier to just rent a car." He didn't want to be on anyone else's timetable. He wanted to say goodbye and then get out of there. Nana knew how much he loved her, and she had a giant family to buzz around her. She didn't need him there. "Where is she?"

"Do you want to relax for a minute?" She gestured toward an empty chair absolutely surrounded by relatives that he hadn't seen in years and hadn't liked much ever. "I could get you something to eat?"

"No," he said, trying to sound gentle. "Thank you. I just really want to see Nana." *And then get out of here*, he silently added. He loved his parents, but he could see them another time, when they weren't surrounded by a mob.

His mom nodded. "Sure. She's so excited to see you."

He doubted she'd have the energy to be excited about anything, but he didn't argue. He followed his mother through the dining room and kitchen and into the back hallway. Years and years ago, these had been servants' quarters. During his childhood, the big back room had been the storage room. His Nana had shoved a lifetime's worth of things "too good to throw away" into this room. As a kid, he hadn't been able to walk through it. Now he barely recognized it. Someone had cleaned it out and turned it into a spacious bedroom, complete with medical bed, tray table, and chairs.

It was a room designed for dying, and it was full of his relatives.

When Nana saw him, her face lit up, and his heart cracked. "Stephen! Come here, sweetheart!"

He did want to go to her. He wanted to wrap his arms around her and breathe in her scent one last time, tell her how much he loved her, and try not to cry more than a grown man should, but he stood frozen in place.

"Shoo, shoo!" She waved to the door. "Everyone out! Stephen's here!"

If she weren't dying, he would have laughed.

No one was offended, and they all got up and filed out. Even his mother left after giving his hand one last squeeze. Someone softly closed the door behind him.

He went to her then and bent to hug her. He was careful, but even beneath his gentle embrace, her fragile form broke his heart. There was so little of her left. She was almost gone.

He kissed her on the cheek and straightened up, not bothering to hide his tears.

"Sit, sit." She pointed to a nearby chair, which he pulled over. She reached for his hand, and he took hers into both of his. He hadn't wanted to see her like this. Selfishly, he hadn't wanted to feel her suffering, feel her fear, have this memory.

And he *could* feel her suffering, but fear? He didn't feel any. She wasn't afraid.

"Thank you for coming," she said. Her voice was weak, but she still sounded very much like herself. And there was still that mischievous sparkle in her eye. She patted his hand. "I know, I know, it's hard to know what to say. You can't say, 'Hey, how ya doin'?' to someone who's dying!" She laughed, which led to a cough.

"I can tell you that I love you, and I can thank you for doing such a good job of loving me." She had taken such good care of him when he was little. She'd been a refuge.

"I do love you. So much." She held her finger up to her pale lips. "Don't tell the others, but you were always my favorite."

He smiled. He'd known this, but her favoritism wasn't really to his credit. It was more like the way someone loves a puppy who's been kicked more than the unkicked puppy.

"You've always been so special, Stephen, and I know we haven't talked much about how and why you're different because I know you don't like talking about it."

He swallowed hard. It was true. He'd talked to her on the phone weekly since he'd first left Maine, and they never talked about anything hard.

"I think this might be my last chance." She winked. "I don't believe in ghosts."

He exhaled slowly. He didn't see why this needed to be discussed at all. He was different from other people in his family, but he didn't think it was worth dissecting. Lots of people didn't fit in with their families.

"You're such a gifted artist, Stephen."

This was kind of her to say, but she didn't know this. She didn't know the first thing about art, and she'd hardly seen any of his. "Don't think your mom's not proud of you. She shows me pictures and articles on the Internet. But that's not even the specialness I want to talk about. Stephen, there are some things about myself that I've never told you. I have told very few people. I told your grandfather, of course. And over the years, I confided in a few pastors, but no one believed me, so I stopped talking about it. And even though I saw the same thing in you, I didn't want to see it. I didn't want to call attention to it because I wanted to protect you." She took a long, shaky breath. "Sorry, give me a second. Let me catch my breath."

In and out, in and out, she breathed slowly and purposefully. Then she continued, "But in these past few months, I've been spending an awful lot of time with God. Draw near to God, and he will draw near to you. That's quite true, I've discovered. And I feel like God has been telling me that I've been wrong. Wrong to push my gift down, wrong to ignore it in you. And just when I realized all of this, I realized that Jeremiah is just like us."

CHAPTER 2

It took Stephen a second to realize who Nana was talking about. "Patrick's kid?"

She nodded. "Patrick's little boy. He reminds me so much of you, it's uncanny."

Stephen's mind was spinning. *Jeremiah is just like us.* Like them, how? Stephen hadn't even known he and Nana shared some significant likeness. What was she talking about?

Did she mean that Patrick's son was having the dreams?

Did she mean that *she* had the dreams?

Or did she just mean that they were all empaths? He had no idea, and he couldn't think of a way to ask that wouldn't make him sound unhinged.

But she wasn't talking anymore. She was waiting. It was his turn to talk.

"Nana, did you used to have ... or do you have really weird dreams?" He winced.

Her thin brows came together in concern. "Not that I remember. Are you having weird dreams?"

Now he was embarrassed. He was being ridiculous. She
hadn't been talking about dreams. "Nana, I'm not sure what
this gift is that you're talking about."

She smiled. "Sure you do. Stephen, you are the most sensitive
person I've ever known. You feel everything. And not only your
own everything, but everyone around you, you feel their every-
things too. I know it's been hard, and I've been praying about it
your whole life."

Lots of people were sensitive. Lots of people were empathic.
He wasn't as special as she believed, but he wasn't going to argue
with a dying woman.

"Before I leave this earth, I wanted to be sure to tell you, please
don't squelch your gift. Don't ignore it. Let it be what it is. Let
God show you what he wants you to see."

He forced a smile he didn't feel. "Okay, Nana."

She squeezed his hand with a strength that surprised him.
"You promise?"

He nodded, not even sure what he was pledging. "I promise."
And then he felt her relief.

"Oh, thank heavens." She laughed and put one frail hand on
her chest. "It's so good to get that off my chest. I was really
nervous to have this little chat. I didn't want to annoy you."

"Oh, Nana. You could never annoy me."

She smiled. "I know you wouldn't do anything to hurt me on purpose, but you can't really control when you're annoyed." She sighed. "So you'll look out for Jeremiah?"

Um, what?

"That's what I'm asking of you, Stephen. I'm going to die. I need you to look after Jeremiah."

"Nana, I live in Nashville." And Jeremiah already had parents. Suddenly he remembered how Patrick had treated him when he was little. "Patrick is nice to his son, isn't he?"

"Oh yes. The boy isn't abused or anything." She was horrified at the suggestion. "I know Patrick can be a bit much, but he wouldn't hurt a fly. Sure, Patrick is a little embarrassed of Jeremiah, calls him a wuss sometimes and tries to toughen him up, but Jeremiah is loved, and his mother is wonderful."

So then what did any of these people need from him?

"But Patrick isn't like you. He's about as sensitive as a two-by-four."

Stephen laughed. "Nana, I live in Nashville," he said again.

"I know. But you can spend the night here tonight, and you can befriend the boy. Get his email address or his online handle or whatever it's called. Keep in touch with him. Let him know that you're available. Just know him. Let him know you. Then he'll have someone safe to talk to."

He didn't want to do this. His life was full and busy. He didn't have time for a new project. And he didn't have a lot of experience with children, nor did he have the desire to change that.

"Please, Stephen. I've never asked you for anything else."

This was true. She had not. He nodded. "Of course, Nana. I don't know what it will look like, but I will make it happen."

"Oh, Stephen, you can't imagine how much peace that gives me." She patted his hand again.

He could imagine, actually. He could feel it.

"I had them make up your bed. Thank you for staying the night. It makes me happy knowing you're within these walls again."

He worked to hide his alarm at that, but she felt it. "What is it? What's wrong?"

"Nothing, Nana. I'm fine. Just ..." How was he supposed to lie to her and get away with it? "I'm just a little overwhelmed."

She studied him. "I know, honey. I'm sorry for that." She glanced at the door. "Go get yourself something to eat. Food always helps, and there's enough of it out there to feed an army. Go meet your cousin, and tell your mother to give me a few minutes alone to nap."

Fear gripped him suddenly. Was she about to die? "Are you sure you want to be alone?"

She nodded. "Tell her just twenty minutes. I'm afraid our little chat has tuckered me out." She glanced at the door. "Go ahead now. Shoo."

He didn't want to leave her, but he did.

He closed the door behind him, delivered the message to his mother in a kitchen crowded with casseroles, and then went into the dining room.

A boy sat at the large oak table all alone, drawing in a sketch pad. Stephen didn't need to be introduced. This was Jeremiah. Stephen sat beside him and watched him draw for a moment.

Interesting. It wasn't half bad. "Nice dragon."

The boy flinched as if the words had stung.

Stephen recognized the reaction—intimately—and his heart softened toward the boy. The kid might be Patrick's son, but that wasn't the kid's fault.

Stephen slid his chair closer and leaned on the table. "Good job with his eyes. Eyes are really hard."

Without moving his head, Jeremiah looked at Stephen. He was so suspicious that Stephen almost laughed.

If it were true that this boy had inherited whatever sensitivity gene had tortured Stephen his whole childhood, then this boy could feel that Stephen wasn't thrilled to be engaging with him.

Stephen concentrated on changing his mood. A minute later, the boy put his pencil down and looked Stephen in the eye.

"I'm Stephen, your father's cousin."

"My name is Jeremiah. I know who you are. You're the artist."

Stephen had enjoyed a few accolades in his career, but this short sentence made him swell with pride more than those public praises had. At least someone in his family knew who he was.

"That's right." He glanced down at the dragon. "And you're an artist too."

Jeremiah's smile was barely perceptible, but it was there. Then it fell away, and he went back to his dragon.

It was exactly how Stephen would have handled the interaction when he was young. It was a lot like how he would have handled it now.

With Nana's words echoing in his brain, Stephen felt pressured to continue the conversation, but he knew that's not what the boy wanted, so he simply sat there silently. He watched his relatives mingling, interacting, and squabbling until that grew old. Then he took out his phone and started answering emails.

For more than an hour he sat beside Jeremiah. No one approached either of them. No one even looked their way. It was as if they were not part of the family.

And that was okay with both of them.

CHAPTER 3

N ana had insisted that Stephen be given his "old room,"
though it was clear that someone else had been staying
in it. Had the favoritism always been this blatant? No wonder
his cousins didn't like him.

It was the biggest guest room, the corner room on the second
floor. Closest to the upstairs bathroom. Four windows. It was a
great room.

Stephen stood on the threshold, not wanting to enter it.

The room was time frozen. The wallpaper was the same. The
rug was the same. Furniture, same. The bedding had to have
been changed, but it was the same color and style.

"What's wrong?" Jeremiah's mother was standing beside
him.

"Hey, Carrie." He was tempted to say, "Your son is cool.
Congratulations" but he didn't. "Nothing's wrong." He quickly stepped into the room to prove this was true. "Just brings

back so many memories." He tried to make this sound like it
was a good thing.

"I'll bet. You spent a lot of time here, didn't you?"

He sighed. "I sure did. But that was a long time ago." He had
managed to stay away for years. And not that he was rushing
Nana's death, but once she left this earth, he would never, ever
return to this house.

He would stay here tonight, and then his obligations were
finished.

He knew he wouldn't be able to fall asleep, so he took a few
sleeping pills. He hoped this would solve two problems at once,
but he woke up at two in the morning, stiff as a board in the
center of his bed, sweating, with his covers cast off.

He gingerly looked around the room, needing to question
where he was but scared to know the answer.

But he was in Nana's ordinary house. In his real room. Nothing to be scared of. And he couldn't remember any tendrils of a
dream, which was great news.

Maybe those nightmares had been a childhood affliction.

Maybe he'd outgrown it.

He was parched.

He got up, put his jeans on so that he wouldn't be wandering around the crowded house in his boxers, and then slipped
downstairs, careful to be quiet. He didn't know how many
people were trying to sleep in that house, but he thought there
were several.

The light from the open refrigerator door lit the small frame of the boy.

Jeremiah jumped when he saw him and slammed the door shut like he'd been caught doing something naughty.

Stephen turned on the light over the stove so they wouldn't be standing there in the dark. "Thirsty, or hungry?" He reached up and opened the cupboard, keeping his eyes on the boy.

"Thirsty," he whispered. And he sounded it.

"Sorry. Didn't mean to scare you."

"You didn't," he lied.

Stephen smiled and re-opened the fridge. "What's your pleasure? Milk? Orange juice?"

"I was going to have soda."

Stephen laughed. "Okay." He handed him a can of Dr. Pepper. "I won't tell."

"Thanks." He popped it open and took a long drink.

Stephen went for the milk. He didn't think a can of sugar would help him fall back asleep.

Jeremiah burped. "Why are you awake?"

Stephen chuckled. "Not sure. Just woke up."

"Did something wake you up?"

A chill raced down Stephen's back. He hesitated. "Why? Did you hear something?"

Slowly, Jeremiah shook his head, his eyes staying locked on Stephen's.

"Are you okay, Jeremiah?"

He stopped shaking his head, but he did not nod.

"You want to watch some TV?"

Jeremiah's face lit up.

"Come on." Stephen started toward the living room. "Let's see what's on." He doubted Nana had Netflix.

"My mom is going to get mad." Jeremiah settled into a plush armchair, clutching his soda.

"You can tell her it's my fault. What do you like to watch?"

"Something not scary."

Stephen grabbed the remote from the coffee table and handed it to the boy. "Here. You pick."

Jeremiah started flipping through the channels. "I don't know what any of these shows are."

Stephen sighed. "Me neither, bud." He didn't watch much TV. He took a long drink of his milk and watched the channels flick by.

Jeremiah stopped on *King of the Hill* and questioned Stephen with his eyes. "Is this okay?"

Stephen didn't care. "Sure is."

Jeremiah pulled an afghan off the back of his chair, snuggled up under it, and gave the cartoon his full attention. Minutes later, Stephen heard soft snoring. Now he wasn't sure what to do. He probably shouldn't leave him and didn't really want to. So he tried to get comfortable.

As the commercials played between episodes, his eyelids fell shut, and his breaths lengthened. The next thing he knew, he was standing in his Nana's living room, fear gripping him like a vice.

To his immediate left, a short set of stairs led down to another level of the house—a level that he knew wasn't really there.

As a boy, he'd spent countless waking hours exploring this house, looking for some secret door or hatch that would lead to that part of the house, but he'd never found it.

Because that part of the house didn't exist.

But yet here he was again, looking at the stairs, and if he went down them, he would be standing in that impossible part of the house.

He scanned the living room, which was still the living room, but things were different. His feet stood on carpet where Nana had hardwood. The digital clock on the wall told him it was ninety-nine minutes past nine. The TV was older, and it was off.

Jeremiah's chair was different, and he wasn't in it. But the afghan still was, curled up in a knot on the armrest.

Stephen squeezed his eyes shut and took a big breath. Then he opened them, hoping things would be back to normal, and knowing they would not be.

It's just a nightmare. Relax. You're not a kid anymore.

His heart pounded, and he was sweating. He took a deep breath. How had he handled this when he was a kid? He'd wandered around, trying to wake up, and then he'd gone back to his bed. Is that what Stephen had to do now? Get back to bed? A desperate desire for that familiar bed overtook him then. He could climb in, pull the covers over his head, and wait till morning. Yes, that's what he'd done back then.

Maybe that's what he should do now.

He looked at the couch behind him. It didn't look nearly as inviting as his bed would be. It didn't look safe. Okay, then, he would just go back to bed—like the old days. If Jeremiah were actually still in that chair, then he'd be fine on his own.

Stephen glanced at the stairs to his left. He didn't need to go down there. He knew that way did not lead to his bedroom. He'd tried that route dozens of times. Sure, it had been years, but he doubted much had changed.

The accuracy of his memory surprised him. It was all coming back to him. He had a clear mental map of the layout. Those stairs led to a carpeted, cramped hallway that led to three small apartments—apartments so big they couldn't possibly fit in Nana's house.

And he knew what lay dead ahead of him too. It looked like Nana's dark dining room, but it wouldn't be. Not really.

In this version of the dining room, there would be a dark stairwell up to a grand hallway that led to a narrow bridge suspended over a giant library that didn't exist.

Just find your bed. Just start moving. If you don't start, you're never going to start.

Heavy feet carried him into the dining room and to the foot of the stairs. He didn't want to touch the banister at all, but he gripped it tightly, afraid the stairs were going to disappear beneath his feet and send him crashing to the floor below.

The stairs did not disappear. They were as solid as any other stairs, and then he was in a dark hallway, but he could see the light ahead. The light of the library.

He walked toward the light.

Sure enough, the library appeared, and it was every bit as grand as he remembered. A room as big as his Nana's entire house, walls lined with bookshelves full of colorful spines.

He could smell the books. They smelled like paper and vanilla with a hint of coffee. They smelled like time. He loved books. He loved the smell of books. But that smell did not bring him comfort right now.

He had to get across the rope bridge that stretched out across the giant room, suspended thirty feet over the floor.

It would sway when he stepped out onto it. The ropes would creak, and he would be terrified. But he would probably get across it, and then he could get back to his bed.

Probably.

He crept to the edge of the bridge and pushed down on it with one foot. He weighed a lot more than he had the last time he'd weight tested this bridge. Would it hold him? Did the laws of physics apply in his nightmare-land?

He remembered then that there was a really fancy lamp over an old desk. He'd always thought it was shaped like a dragon, spitting out the light like fire. He glanced to his left and down to see if the lamp and desk were still there.

They were, the light shining as brightly as he remembered.

How was that possible? How could his memory be so accurate?

The lamp bore an uncanny resemblance to the dragon Jeremiah had been drawing. He shook his head. *Stop dillydallying. Get back to your room.*

He stepped onto the bridge and waited for the sound of snapping brackets or fraying ropes, but there was no sound.

He crossed it quickly, enduring the sway, not looking down, trying not to wonder why any library would have a walking bridge stretched out across the middle of it, trying not to wonder about any of this.

He reached the other side safely and took a deep breath. He turned and gave the grand room one last look. He didn't like the library, didn't want to visit it, but it sure was beautiful. "Adios," he whispered. This was his last time here. He was sure of it.

He turned and headed into the dark hallway, the same one he'd traversed so many times before. The peeling wallpaper; the spongy, creaking floor; and the cobwebs were every bit as terrifying as they'd been back then.

Third door on the left. Third door on the left.

He hurried toward it, flung open the door, and nearly fell inside. Then he hurried to get into the bed that was almost like his bed and then pull the covers up over his body. *It's just a dream. You'll wake up soon. It's just a dream.*

CHAPTER 4

S tephen woke with a start and sat up.

Ouch. His neck was as stiff as a rock. He reached up to rub it and looked around his Nana's living room, which was blessedly empty. Sunlight poured in through the windows. He'd slept too late.

He looked at Jeremiah's chair, empty except for the balled-up afghan.

He closed his eyes and rubbed them. He had to get out of here. He would say goodbye to Nana, give Jeremiah his phone number, and then he was getting out of this house once and for all.

He had no idea why this house gave him a recurring nightmare, but it did, just like he'd feared it would, and he was done.

He took the steps two at a time and went into his room to make his bed. Then he shoved his few belongings into his bag and slung it over his shoulder.

He ran back down the stairs, dropped his bag by the door, and spun to go say his goodbyes.

The dining room was packed.

"Hey, sleepyhead," his sister said.

"Hey, Trish. Nice to see you." He scanned the room for Jeremiah and found him in the same seat at the dining room table with the same sketch pad in front of him. But this time he wasn't looking at his dragon. He was staring at Stephen with wide eyes. Stephen couldn't imagine why, but the boy was excited.

Stephen smiled at him. "Be right back," he mouthed, and then he headed to the kitchen, intending to cut through it and get to Nana's room.

But Jeremiah followed him. "Hey!" he whispered.

Stephen continued through the kitchen and into the back hallway before stopping. He turned to look down at his young friend.

"You were there," the boy said in wonder.

Stephen's skin broke out in goosebumps. "I was where?"

"How were you there?"

"Where?" he almost snapped.

"I saw you."

"Saw me where?" He did snap.

Jeremiah flinched.

"Sorry. Didn't mean to be short. I haven't had my coffee yet. Where did you see me?"

"In the library."

Stephen stopped breathing.

Nana's house didn't have a library.

At least, her real one didn't.

"You want to go outside for a minute?" Stephen asked, trying to keep his voice even.

Jeremiah glanced at the back door. "I think it's kind of cold out."

Stephen sighed. "I know. It's just for a minute." He nodded toward the door. "Come on." He could not risk someone overhearing the conversation they were about to start. They'd both be committed.

Jeremiah followed him outside, across the cluttered driveway to the old, rusted swing that hadn't been rusty the last time Stephen had sat in it.

They both sat. Yep. It was cold. He wouldn't keep the boy out here for long. "Tell me what you mean by the library."

He frowned and crossed his arms in front of him. "You were above me, on the bridge. In my dream. You were really there, right?"

A crushing weight on Stephen's chest made him fear suffocation. What was going on? How was this possible? And out of the thousand questions that tried to push their way out of Stephen's mouth, the one that won the race was: "How did you get to the floor of the library?"

The boy stared at him for several seconds and then smiled, a hint of mischief glinting in his eyes. He had Nana's eyes. "You don't know how to get to the library?"

How was this conversation happening? How had Jeremiah seen him in his dream?

Because it wasn't a dream.

Yes, it was.

What else could it have been?

"Have you ever been into the bedroom with the purple bedspread?" Jeremiah asked matter-of-factly.

A wave of sickness washed over Stephen. He gripped the rusty chain of the swing so hard that it hurt his hand. That purple bedspread had been there fourteen years ago. And it was still there. Now living in Jeremiah's imagination.

Somehow.

"No, I haven't, but I know the one you mean." The purple bedspread was on the bed in apartment number three. "I know where it is, but I've never gone into that room."

"Well, if you go into the bathroom there, there's a door into the library."

Unbelievably, Stephen felt a pang of jealousy. He'd never been to the library. He'd only hovered above it. He forced himself to breathe. *Don't be ridiculous.*

"It's a cool door. It's actually two doors. They swing and don't touch the floor, like the ones on the cowboy shows."

Oh, of course. Why wouldn't saloon doors lead into a giant library? "Jeremiah, how many times have you had this dream?"

He shrugged. "I don't know. A lot. Most nights that I'm here." He wasn't as scared as he should be. He was being rather pragmatic about the whole thing. Why wasn't he more scared? Stephen had endured these dreams when he was the same age, and he'd been terrified.

"Jeremiah!" Carrie cried from the back porch. "What are you doing out here? I was scared to death!"

Oh, really? You *were scared?*

"It's too cold out here! Jeremiah, you come here this instant!"

Jeremiah gave him an apologetic look and then got up and trudged toward his mother, who was glaring at Stephen, her eyes full of judgment.

CHAPTER 5

Carrie took Jeremiah out to run errands, so Stephen didn't see him again until after lunch. The wait felt long. He wanted to talk to Nana, but she was sleeping, and her security guards kept shooing him away. He didn't want to go anywhere near his bedroom, so he took his laptop out and sat in Jeremiah's drawing chair at the dining room table.

He tried to answer work emails but couldn't concentrate and instead found himself typing "dream sharing" into the search bar, which quickly taught him that if such a thing existed, it was not called "dream sharing."

Instead, he found information about "lucid dreaming," a phrase that sounded completely wacko to him, and "mutual dreaming," which rang a little closer to true. He couldn't bring himself to believe that this was a real thing, and yet he couldn't stop himself from reading about it.

Science, as one would expect, claimed there was no such thing. But some websites argued otherwise. Not surprising since the world wide web also had dozens of sites dedicated to Chupacabra sightings.

"Meshing dreams" were dreams that shared the same elements. That wasn't what this was. Jeremiah seeing him in the library wasn't an "element" of a dream. It *was* the dream. Then there was a "meeting dream" in which two people meet and communicate inside the dream. He hadn't communicated with Jeremiah, but he had a feeling that if he'd seen him and tried, he would have been able to. A doctor in Albuquerque was studying mutual dreaming in hopes of proving that the dream world is in fact an alternate reality—

Stephen slammed his laptop shut. This was too much. There was no such thing as an alternate reality. He had to get a grip. There had to be another explanation. He closed his eyes and concentrated.

Maybe he'd talked in his sleep while he was sleeping on the couch. Maybe he'd said something about the library or the bridge, and Jeremiah had heard him. If this were the case, then that meant that little Jeremiah was at least a liar and possibly a sociopath.

But he knew this wasn't true. If Jeremiah had been lying, Stephen probably would have been able to tell.

He had to get out of this house. He jumped up, grabbed his jacket, headed outside, and started walking. He took deep breaths of sharp, crisp Maine air. The movement made him feel better. It clarified nothing, of course, but it made him feel better. When he was far enough away from the house that he could manage it, he started to pray. *God, if you're there ...*

He stopped, thinking about what to say.

Stephen didn't know whether he believed in God. He hadn't grown up going to church. He'd always known that Nana believed in all of that Christian stuff, and she'd read him Bible stories when he was little, but that was the entirety of his religious training. But if he was honest with himself, there had been moments over the course of his life when he'd believed God was real because he'd *felt* him. He'd felt something like him, anyway—some*one* close by, invisible, powerful.

But those moments had been so few and far between that it was easy to talk himself out of them altogether. And despite all his many emotions, Stephen was still a rational being. He hadn't seen much evidence of God over the years. And why would something so powerful as God hide himself so efficiently?

God, he tried again, *I need your help. If you're real, then this could be real too.* His breath caught. He'd just had a mini epiphany: If God was real, then he was, by definition, a supernatural being, and that opened the door to the supernatural.

He shook his head. He didn't want any part of any of this.

If God was real, he and the whole supernatural world could exist without Stephen.

He stopped walking and looked back at the house. He could just leave. He'd grown up and turned out just fine despite weird childhood dreams. Jeremiah would too. He could drive away, go back to his life. Leave well enough alone.

He wanted to do exactly that, and yet he knew he wouldn't. He wouldn't leave Jeremiah.

A red minivan pulled into Nana's driveway, and Stephen headed back that way. He didn't know what Carrie drove, but she seemed like the red minivan type.

Jeremiah was sitting on the front steps when he got there.

He sat beside him. "Does your mother know you're out here? It's still pretty chilly." But at least he had a jacket on this time.

Jeremiah shrugged. "I don't know."

"Maybe you should go back inside, then. Don't want you to get in trouble." And he didn't want to be blamed.

"You're the only one who likes me."

The words stung, and the sting felt familiar. "Yeah." Stephen rubbed his hands together. "You can feel it, huh?"

"Yeah."

Stephen could feel it too. When he was around someone who didn't care for him, he could literally feel their dislike. When this happened with a crowd of people who disliked him, it could be mighty uncomfortable. "They just don't understand us. We don't fit in. But the life I live now, I'm surrounded by people who like me. It's just hard because we don't get to pick our families. We don't get to pick who we grow up around. But I promise you, it can get better."

"That's good news." Jeremiah's spirit lifted.

"Can I ask you a weird question?"

"Yeah!" Jeremiah was excited. He liked weird questions.

"Have you had that kind of dream in other houses?"

Slowly, Jeremiah turned and looked at him. He was studying him. "Have you?"

Stephen shook his head. "I have not."

Jeremiah sighed. "Me neither."

"So what is it about this house?" Stephen muttered, not expecting an answer.

"I don't know. You're the grownup here."

Stephen laughed. "I suppose that's true, but until you said that you saw me in the library, I really thought that library was just something I invented in my subconscious imagination."

Jeremiah's head snapped toward him. "For real?"

"For real. I thought it was just a dream. A scary one, and one I had over and over for some reason. But yes, just a dream." He still hoped that were true.

Jeremiah stared at him like he was stupid. "They're not just dreams."

"Yeah. I'm starting to wonder if that's the case. Can I ask you another question?"

He sat up straighter and nodded proudly.

"Why aren't you more scared? I mean, these rooms that we see, some of them are pretty scary."

"I used to be more scared, but I got used to it. The hallway right outside our bedrooms is the scariest part. And the back stairs. I try to stay away from those places. But the rest of it isn't so bad. I like exploring."

Nana hadn't been completely right when she'd said that he and Jeremiah were the same. There was some courage swimming around in Jeremiah's gene pool.

Maybe he'd gotten it from his mother.

"You shouldn't be scared," Jeremiah said.

"I'll try not to be. But I don't like things I can't explain."

Jeremiah stared at him. "Why do you have to explain it?"

"I don't know. I just do."

CHAPTER 6

Jeremiah helped Stephen dry the dishes and put them away. When they finished, they found themselves alone in the kitchen with nothing else to do.

"Do you know how much longer you're staying here?" Stephen asked.

"Till she dies, I think."

What an unfair situation. This kid didn't need to be trapped in this house. Whether or not he was scared of these dreams, or whatever they were, he deserved to get a good night's sleep.

"Do you want to go home?"

He nodded. "I miss my cat. And my bed."

"Okay, then." Stephen tossed the dish towel onto the counter. "Let's go find your mom."

Jeremiah looked confused, but he didn't argue.

Carrie was in the living room with a spattering of her in-laws.

None of them looked up when Jeremiah and Stephen walked in.

Stephen pushed an ottoman closer to Carrie and sat down on it.

Now she looked up, saw Jeremiah, and held a hand out to him. He went to her, and she pulled him onto the couch beside her. The gesture was protective.

"I was thinking," Stephen said, unsure how to say what he had to say and even more unsure of how to say it convincingly. "You and Jeremiah don't need to stay. I can stay and help Trish"—He glanced at his sister, who looked stunned—"with Nana."

Carrie looked suspicious.

"I appreciate all you've done, but she's not even your family, and—"

"Patrick has asked me to be here and to help."

Stephen understood the literal meaning of her words, but he also heard a second message loud and clear: She didn't want to go home. She would rather be here caring for a dying woman than home with her husband. Stephen couldn't blame her. Patrick was one annoying individual, but her reluctance to spend time with her spouse was bad news for Jeremiah. Stephen glanced at the boy, who didn't look surprised by any of this. He knew exactly what Stephen was trying to do, and he'd probably known that it would fail.

"But what about school? Doesn't Jeremiah need to get back—"

"He's homeschooled." She said this defensively, expecting an argument from him. This was strange, since he didn't even know her. Did she usually endure criticism from strangers?

"I was picked on," Jeremiah explained. "There were lots of bullies—"

His mother shushed him, and Stephen held up his hands. "No judgment here. I don't care where he goes to school." He tried to think of another argument, but he couldn't, and the moment grew increasingly awkward. "Okay." He slid the ottoman back and stood.

Jeremiah started to get up too, but his mother pulled him back down. "Stay right here for a minute." She looked at Stephen suspiciously.

Stephen backed out of the room, almost bumping into his sister in the dining room.

"Did you mean it?" she asked.

"Mean what?"

"Did you mean it that you'll take a shift here? Taking care of Nana?"

"Trish, how many people does it really take?"

"Do it for a few days, and you'll see."

He was racked with guilt. He'd been willing to do this for Jeremiah, but he wasn't willing to do it for his sister? "Sure. I can stay for a few days."

"Awesome." She gave him a quick, tight hug. "Thank you. I've got a zillion things I need to do at home. But I'll check in soon, okay? And if you need anything, call." Trish bustled around and then was on her way to the door. "You sure you're okay?"

He nodded. He did have a life and a job to get back to, and supernatural weirdness to get away from, but sure, he was okay.

"Great." She gave him another hug and then nearly ran out the door.

Stephen took his time making some tea and then took it into the living room and sat in a wing chair. "Jeremiah already go to bed?" He'd expected to find him there in front of the TV.

Carrie eyed him suspiciously. "I know we don't know each other, so please don't be offended by this, but I'm uncomfortable with how much attention you're paying to my son."

All of the sympathy he'd felt for this woman for being married to Patrick was gone in a second. "How could that possibly not be offensive? He's family. And I'm a nice person. Nice people are usually nice to family."

"Fine." Her jaw set, she got up and left the room.

He watched her go, glad for her absence.

He gave her time to get settled into her room so that he didn't accidentally encounter her in the hallway. He checked in on Nana, who was sleeping peacefully, and then he too went upstairs. He intended to play on his phone all night, so he didn't even take off his jeans.

It was harder to stay awake than he'd thought it would be, but he was still managing when the door to his room flew open, and a wild-eyed Jeremiah filled the frame, breathing hard. "Have you seen her?"

"Seen who, your mom?"

"No! The woman tied to the chair!"

Goosebumps broke out on Stephen's arms and neck. "What are you talking about?"

"She's in the metal room." He stepped closer. "We have to help her."

The metal room? Stephen didn't know about any metal room. "Your mom and Nana are the only people in this house, bud. There's no one else."

He shook his head furiously. "She's not one of us. I don't know her. I've never seen her because I've never been in the metal room until night."

Stephen stared at him for a moment, processing. "I'm sorry that you got scared, and I don't know how to explain what you saw, but I promise you that there's no one else in this house."

Jeremiah shook his head. "She's there. And she's trapped."

CHaPTer 7

Trapped? Someone was trapped in Jeremiah's dream? Stephen couldn't quite wrap his mind around that. "What do you mean, she's trapped?"

"Come on! We've got to help her."

What did Jeremiah expect him to do, exactly? He stared at the boy stupidly.

"I can't help her by myself." His voice quivered.

"What, do you want me to fall asleep right now and help you?"

"Yes! I was waiting for you!"

Oh boy. What was he supposed to do here? "Okay, I'll try to go to sleep, but no promises. And you definitely need to go back to bed." *Before your mother catches you in here.*

"You'll really try?"

Stephen sighed. "Yes, I'll really try. Now go to bed."

Jeremiah was seriously unsettled.

"You want me to walk you back to your room?"

He backed up a step. "No, I can do it. I'm not a baby."

"Okay, then. See you on the other side." He watched Jeremiah disappear into the shadows and then lay back on his pillow. How was he supposed to fall asleep on demand? His body was as stiff as a board. His mind spun.

A third person? In their dream world? How?

And why was Jeremiah so sure this was going to work? He'd seen him in the library once. It didn't mean they could just go on dream missions together. *You just told him that you'd see him on the other side.* Yep, he had. So it didn't matter whether this was going to work. He still had to try.

He tried to slow his breathing, concentrating on nothingness.

But sleep never found him. When twilight cast his room in shades of gray, he tried to tell himself it wasn't morning yet, but the light grew stronger and stronger until he gave up and sat up.

He'd failed. And he was exhausted.

He peeked into Jeremiah's room on his way by. The boy was curled up in a ball, sound asleep. He wondered if he should wake him. It was early, but if the boy was wandering around the dream house looking for him, maybe he could relieve him of that waiting.

He pulled his head out of the room and used some extra oomph to shut the door. It wasn't quite a slam, but he hoped it might stir Jeremiah toward waking.

Stephen went downstairs and checked on Nana, who was still sleeping. He made himself some coffee and then scrolled through the news on his phone until he heard footsteps on the stairs.

Jeremiah peeked down at him over the banister.

"Good morning."

The kid scowled.

"I'm really sorry. I couldn't fall asleep."

Jeremiah eyed the mug in his hands. "Maybe you should quit coffee."

Stephen chuckled. "Maybe." He waited for him to come closer before asking, "Did you dream again?"

Jeremiah shook his head. "I don't know why."

Thank goodness. Stephen hadn't abandoned him in dream-world.

"We need to try again tonight."

Stephen tipped his head back and closed his eyes. How could he solve a problem that didn't actually exist? "Remind me why you think that she needs our help?"

Slowly, as if talking to a dunce, Jeremiah said, "She's ... tied ... to ... a ... chair."

Oh yeah. That.

"And she's crying. And she was so excited to see me. I don't think she's seen anyone in a long time."

A chill raced down his spine. "Jeremiah, have you ever told your mother that this house gives you nightmares?"

"They're not nightmares," he said quickly, and then he added, more quietly, "and yes, I've told her."

"And what did she say?"

"She told me to pray before I went to sleep, that God would protect me from bad dreams."

Oh boy.

"I told her that they weren't dreams, and she said they were, so I stopped telling her. And I have prayed. I have prayed a lot."

Stephen didn't want to talk about prayer. Not now. Not with Jeremiah. "So where is this metal room?"

Jeremiah pointed toward Nana's bedroom.

Stephen's eyes followed his pointing, trying to remember what that area of the house looked like when he was asleep, but he couldn't picture it. "Hang on. Give me a second." He closed his eyes. Had he ever gone through the kitchen and into that back hallway? He didn't think so. At least, he couldn't remember doing it. He opened his eyes to meet Jeremiah's patiently staring back.

"What's the room look like?"

"It's full of metal. And boxes."

That didn't sound remotely familiar.

Carrie came into the living room, startling them both. "We're all out of coffee creamer." She eyed his mug accusingly.

"Would you like me to go get more?"

"That would be very nice of you." She looked at her son. "Come on. Let's get breakfast."

Stephen stood, stretched, and headed for the door.

CHAPTER 8

S tephen was so glad to be out of the house that he took his sweet time fetching the coffee creamer. And maybe he was being a little passive aggressive too. Carrie could drink her coffee black this time. He felt bad thinking such petty thoughts, but his guilt gave him an idea. Maybe he should try to be more obnoxious. If he were more obnoxious than Patrick, then Carrie would go home to Patrick, right? And this would get Jeremiah out of that house.

But what about the woman? an obnoxious voice silently asked.

There was no way that woman could be real. If she was, then Stephen would have to be the one to rescue her. He rolled his eyes. How preposterous.

Nana was priority number one. Then Jeremiah. This woman, whatever she was, was pretty far down on the list.

By the time he got back to the house, he was resolute, but as he pulled into the driveway, a heaviness wafted out of the house at him. Grief. Something was wrong. Nana.

He scrambled out of the car and hurried inside to find everyone in tears. His mother flung her arms around him. He hugged her tightly, absorbing her grief.

She stepped back and wiped at her eyes. "Good heavens ..." She chuckled ruefully. "I knew it was coming, so why does this hurt so bad?"

"In part because you are exhausted. And also, you loved her, and she's gone. We try to prepare ourselves, but we can't. Not really. What can I do to help?"

She shrugged. "I don't think there's anything to do. All the arrangements have already been made or are being made." She shrugged. "You can speak at the funeral if you want—"

He most definitely did not want that.

"But other than that, I guess there's not much for you to do until then. I'm not sure when the service will be yet, but I'm thinking probably next weekend. We're still trying to figure that out."

He nodded. "Okay. Let me know." The longer he was away from work, the more of a mess he'd find when he got back, but that was okay. Nana was more important, and this was the last time he was going to miss work for her. This realization packed a punch that he was unprepared for. He needed to sit down. He put the creamer in the fridge, and someone immediately pulled it out. The house was filling up fast. He should have gotten more creamer.

He went into the living room and found a spot on the end of the couch. His eyes found Jeremiah's sweet, cherubic face, which offered him a sad smile.

Stephen sat there, still, not knowing what to do with himself. The grief hurt, and he wasn't on board with fully experiencing that grief just yet. Not with all these people around. Not here. He took his phone out to distract himself but then felt guilty and shoved it back into his pocket. No one else had their phones out.

So he sat there with everyone else. It felt like a waiting room, but he didn't know what they were waiting for. Nightfall? The funeral? For the grief to go away?

His caffeine-energy wore off, and he sank deeper into the cushions. He tipped his head back and stared at the ceiling. It was too warm in this room. Who had cranked up the heat?

He let his eyes drift shut, knowing he wouldn't fall asleep, not under these conditions, and then minutes later, when he realized he was in fact drifting too close to neverland, he sat up with a start—

in a cold, empty room. He groaned. *Wake up!* he snapped at himself. He slapped himself across the face, harder than he meant to, and it smarted, but he was still in the cold, dark room.

Why was it dark? He couldn't have possibly slept all day, especially not on the couch in a crowded room. He turned to look at the window behind him, which was covered in old newspapers that had been painted black. He could make out small cracks of light trying to get through, but it wasn't enough to light the room.

He had to figure out a way to wake up. He couldn't be asleep in the living room in front of all his grieving relatives. They already thought he was a weirdo. This would be the icing on the cake—just the thing they needed to focus on to distract them from their own grief and fear of death.

He pinched himself on the arm, hard, knowing it wouldn't do any good, and it didn't. It hurt, sure enough, but it didn't wake him up.

Then he remembered the woman in the chair.

Still trying to figure out a way to wake up, he started toward the kitchen.

Then a thought stopped him cold in his tracks, and he slowly turned toward the front door.

When he was little, had he ever tried to *leave* the house? He couldn't remember, but he probably hadn't because the outside world was a lot scarier when one was little. But now, now he didn't need to be afraid to go outside by himself. He was an adult. Adults did that all the time.

His curiosity overpowered his concern for the possibly imaginary woman, and he reached for the doorknob. Then, half expecting the sky to be dark and filled with winged monsters, he opened the door.

CHAPTER 9

The sky was not black.

There were no monsters.

This was his grandmother's yard. Nana's driveway. There was his rental, right where he'd left it after his creamer run. There was his sister's car. There was Carrie's minivan.

He stepped further outside so he could see the neighbors' houses, which were right where they were supposed to be.

If he were to go into one of them, would their floor plan be all wacky too?

He stepped back inside. He didn't have time to wonder such things. He had to wake up. Also, more pressing than the neighbors' supernatural floor plans was the possibility of a woman in the other end of the house.

"Wake up, wake up, wake up," he said loudly as he headed toward the kitchen. He stomped his feet, hoping that might do something.

The only thing it did was cause him heel pain.

A lit lantern sat on the wood stove in Nana's kitchen, which looked a lot like Nana's kitchen was supposed to look, except that the ceiling was too high. Freakishly high, in fact. It was more than twice the height of a normal ceiling. It seemed the weak light from the lantern was struggling to reach it.

"Get this over with," he muttered and stepped out into the back hallway.

It was way too long. He was in the middle of it, but it stretched out in both directions for more than a hundred feet. The hallway was lined with doors, and they were all shut.

He held his breath and listened.

Suddenly, he was very, very freaked out.

He didn't think he'd ever been in this part of the house, and he didn't think he was alone. *What are you listening for, exactly?* he asked himself.

He didn't know. Something. Anything.

Something that would tell him that she was really there. Anything that would tell him something.

"It's that one."

Stephen jumped and whirled around to see Jeremiah standing in the hallway. "What are you doing here?"

"Why are you whispering?" Was that amusement on his face? Not so cherubic now.

"We have to hurry." Jeremiah stepped closer to the door. "Someone will wake you up soon."

Stephen stopped him with a hand on his shoulder. "Why are you asleep?"

"I saw that you fell asleep," he said impatiently, "so I ran upstairs and went to bed."

"You can do that?" Fall asleep on demand? That fast? Without fear?

"I had to." In one fluid motion, he shook off Stephen's hand, turned the knob, and pushed the door open.

Stephen gasped.

What he was looking at made absolutely no sense.

The door opened on a giant room, and sure enough, its floor and walls were made of metal. The door was centered, and the room had to be sixty feet wide. The walls did not meet the floor at ninety-degree angles. Instead, they curved out and away, like they'd been stretched.

The room narrowed as it deepened, until the two walls met each other at a sharp angle.

Suddenly he realized what he was looking at.

He was inside the bow of a ship.

He'd never been inside the bow of a ship—and that wasn't the right word, was it? Didn't the inside of a bow have its own name, foreship, or forebow, or something—but that's what this was. He spun around and looked behind him. How had he gotten onto a ship? But it was the same door and the same dark hallway behind him.

"Come on!" Jeremiah said impatiently, pulling on his hand.

The second Stephen's foot hit the steel floor—or was it a deck—it was in motion. His arms flew out to his sides for balance, ripping his hand out of Jeremiah's clutch. Stephen widened his stance and then stood there, trying to evaluate the subtle movement he was feeling.

The ship was rocking.

The ship that didn't exist and couldn't possibly fit in Nana's house was rocking in waters that were not beneath him.

He felt sick, and it wasn't from the motion. What *was* this, and how was Jeremiah taking it all in stride?

"She's over here! Come *on*!"

Stephen's shaky legs carried him toward Jeremiah, toward the center of the room, where giant wooden crates were stacked ten feet high. Some of them were strapped to the floor. He stepped around one of these stacks and then another, and then he stopped cold in his tracks.

There she was. And she wasn't a woman.

She was just a girl.

CHAPTER 10

The woman in the chair looked like she was in high school.

Stephen staggered back a step. He didn't understand what he was seeing. How was this possible?

Desperate eyes looked at him over the thick piece of dirty fabric tied around her head, across her mouth. He could see why Jeremiah had thought she was older. She was wearing a ton of makeup, and her tears had made a mess of it, making her eyes look like two burnt holes in a cream-colored blanket. Her pale skin was sharpened by her dark, dark hair, which was a tangled mess of snarls.

She wore a faded black shirt with a large purple butterfly on the front. The glitter on the butterfly's wings seemed incredibly out of place here. Some of it had fallen off onto her ripped blue jeans, which were tucked into work boots. Dirty, fraying rope secured her arms to the armrests.

The chair was bolted to the floor.

"What do we do?" Jeremiah asked.

It pained Stephen how much Jeremiah was looking to him for leadership, how much he was expecting Stephen to fix this, to even know how to fix this, to even be able to begin to fix this, to even know what *this* was.

"I don't know," Stephen said with difficulty.

"Hurry. You're going to wake up."

The reality of this hit him with a painful force. The kid was right. They had to do something. The clock was ticking. It had been ticking for a while it seemed, but now it was picking up speed. His relatives weren't going to let him sleep on the couch indefinitely. And pretty soon, he wasn't going to have a reason to sleep in this house at all. He had to figure out what he was looking at, and if this was a real person—which it certainly seemed to be—then he had to get her out of here.

He took one tentative step closer, and she flinched.

He held up both hands, palms out. "Sorry, I don't know what to do here, but I promise we do not want to hurt you. We want to help. I'm going to try to take your gag out."

She nodded quickly.

He couldn't read her the way he could most people—as if the whole situation wasn't unsettling enough. Of course he could see that she was scared and uncomfortable, but he couldn't *feel* those things.

Maybe that was a good thing.

"You can't take her gag out," Jeremiah said, but his protest didn't really register. Stephen had no idea what step number two was going to be, but he was pretty sure that he could untie a rag.

He traveled around to the back of her head to get a look. The rag was so tight that he didn't dare try to slip it up over her head or down over the bottom half of her jaw. The knot looked manageable. He could untie that.

But when he reached out, his hand passed right through the fabric. He didn't even feel it. This gave him the strangest sensation, almost like seasickness, but the boat was hardly moving. He moved his hand down to her shoulder, but it passed right through her. He couldn't feel her, and judging by the fact that she hadn't moved, she couldn't feel him either.

Are you the ghost, or am I? Which one of us isn't really here? That question scared him more than anything had thus far. He looked at Jeremiah, who said, point blank, "I told you."

"What does that mean? Why can't I touch her?"

"I don't know."

Of course he didn't know. He was an amazing kid, but he wasn't an expert in alternate dimensions.

Stephen came around to face her. "You can hear me, right?"

She nodded.

"I tried to untie you, and I can't. I can't touch you." He stepped closer and brought his hand down toward her knee, and she flinched again. "I'm not going to hurt you. Just let me show you." Holding one hand up like he was trying to stay a horse, he brought the other one down slowly, gently to her knee—and it passed right through it.

Her face twisted in anguish, and her body made the exact motion of someone crying out—but he didn't hear anything.

"I don't think I can hear you. Can you try to make a noise?"

Nothing happened.

"I didn't hear anything. Did you just try?"

She nodded quickly, her panic growing.

"Can you try again? Make a loud noise."

She closed her eyes in concentration, and her body moved, but he didn't hear anything. She opened her eyes to question him—and then everything went gray and fuzzy, and his stomach rolled with sickness. He blinked and tried to focus and saw his sister leaning over him.

Oh no. He'd manage to tip over on the couch. He sat up quickly and looked around wildly for Jeremiah.

"I told everyone that you've been up all night, tried to shut them up, but you know how they are."

He nodded and sat up quickly, rubbing his eyes. "I'm so sorry." He stood and started toward the stairs.

"Where are you going?" She was suspicious.

"Nowhere," he lied. "Just need to get the cobwebs out."

She wasn't buying it, but she didn't argue.

He took the stairs two at a time and hurried to Jeremiah's room. He didn't knock first; he just barged in.

The boy lay still on top of his covers, sound asleep.

Now that he was here, Stephen wondered what exactly he'd been rushing to do. Wake him up? Maybe he wasn't safe in there. What if the ship took off, separated from the house?

He shook his head. Was that an insane worry? Maybe. How was he supposed to know what was and wasn't insane right now?

Maybe he should let the boy sleep. Maybe Jeremiah would be able to figure something out.

Or maybe he should try to go back to sleep.

He knew it wouldn't work, but he had to try.

He hurried to his room, shoved a chair under the doorknob to keep anyone from interfering this time, lay down, and pressed his eyes shut. "Please God, let me fall asleep."

He tried to relax. He tried not to think about anything. He tried to be tired.

He'd never been so awake in his life.

"Please God," he said again. "He's in there." He didn't know what else to say. If God was real, he knew what Stephen meant.

As the minutes dragged by, he grew more hopeless. He was not going to fall asleep.

Jeremiah was on his own.

"Help him, God," he whispered, and someone knocked on the door. He opened his eyes and looked. The doorknob turned, but the door didn't open. There was a chair in the way.

Stephen got up and moved it. He opened the door to find Jeremiah standing there. Relief flooded through him. "What did I miss?"

He shrugged. "Nothing."

"Nothing? Nothing else happened?"

Jeremiah shook his head. "I tried to talk to her, but she was so scared." He shrugged. "I think she got more scared when you disappeared. It looked like a magic trick. *Poof*, you were gone. I knew you'd woken up, but I didn't know how to explain that to her. I prayed for her, and she looked annoyed. And then I guess I got kind of scared too, so I woke up. Why is she in there?"

"I don't know."

"How are we going to get her out?"

"I don't know that either."

CHAPTER 11

Stephen assumed that, now that Nana had died, Carrie and Jeremiah would be going home. Carrie had no reason to stay anymore, right? But she was in no hurry to leave.

She bumped into him in the kitchen. "Are you staying here tonight?"

"I thought I would. Beats going to a hotel." It didn't, but she might believe the lie.

She nodded contemplatively. "Good. I guess it's silly, but it just seems like the house shouldn't be empty."

This house is not empty.

She was waiting for him to say something. He had nothing to say.

"So I guess we'll head out. I don't know what happens next." She looked defeated. She didn't want to go home. "I'll go find Jeremiah."

He watched her walk away, unsure how to feel. Disappointed? He was losing his partner. Relieved. His partner could go home and get a good night's sleep in complete safety. Worried. About the mystery girl whom he couldn't hear or touch.

He caught Jeremiah on his way down the stairs. He flashed a smile he did not feel, trying to lighten the mood.

Jeremiah did not buy it.

"Hey, you're going to get some actual sleep tonight."

"I don't want to leave."

"I know. But it'll be okay."

"Are you still going to help her?"

Stephen nodded. "I'm going to try." He handed him a business card. "Here is my phone number and email address. You can call or write anytime."

He took the card, surprised.

Stephen squeezed his small shoulder. "I like you. It's cool to have a relative I like."

Jeremiah laughed, and this made Stephen very happy. He got the impression that the boy didn't laugh much.

"Jeremiah!" Carrie called. "Let's go!"

Jeremiah moved around him to go down the stairs, dragging his small suitcase behind him. *Bump, bump, bump,* it clunked down the stairs. Nana would've hated that abuse of her steps, but Nana was beyond worrying about that stuff now.

The door shut, and the house fell silent.

It was the eeriest silence that Stephen had ever heard.

Despite his love for Nana, he'd never wanted to be in this house. He wanted it less now than he ever had.

He wandered around the house, looking for some sign of something amiss, something supernatural, some sort of clue as to why strange things were happening here, why there were extra rooms when he was asleep, why there were strangers tied up in metal rooms.

He took out his phone and looked up the word for the inside of a bow.

Forepeak. Of course. He tucked his phone back into his pocket and stared at the wall. *Are you a wall? And if not, what are you, really?* He was losing his mind.

This was just a house.

A big, old, clean, lived-in house.

Was he going to be able to fall asleep? He was worried that he wouldn't, that he would lie awake all night staring at a dark ceiling, asking it if it were really a ceiling.

He needed to get some exercise. That would help. He grabbed his wallet and left the house. It was at least a mile to the grocery store, and he felt conspicuous with every step. This made him walk faster, and it felt good to get his blood pumping.

In the store he bought some bread, turkey, and chamomile tea—a recipe for slumber.

Then in the checkout line he decided he also needed a king-sized package of Reese's Cups. This would not help his sleep efforts, but he thought it might help alleviate some of his emotional turmoil. He asked for a plastic bag and was told rather unceremoniously that he couldn't have one. So he had to carry a clunky paper bag all the way home. Still, somewhere between the rude cashier and Nana's house, he felt himself relax a little. So what if he was losing his mind? So what if his Nana's house had extra rooms and ghosts? It was all going to be okay.

He didn't know why he suddenly felt this. Dopamine was a powerful thing.

He watched two episodes of *Parenthood*, ate two turkey sandwiches, and then watched a third episode while he ate his candy and drank his tea. And lo and behold, he started to feel sleepy. He didn't want to go up to his creepy bedroom, and he'd recently learned that there was nothing magical about that bedroom. He could fall asleep anywhere in this strange house and still find his way into a nightmare.

He lay down and pulled an afghan up over his shoulders. It smelled like Nana, and this made him sad. He started a fourth episode, and when his eyelids grew heavy and hot, he let them drift shut.

The quiet woke him. He opened his eyes to see why the TV wasn't playing anymore, and the TV was an old one, and it was off.

His gut dropped a few feet before he remembered that this time, this was what he wanted. He threw the afghan off and went straight to the kitchen, through it, and into the back hallway. He paused briefly in front of the door that he knew would open into the bow—no, forepeak—of a ship. He took a breath and opened the door.

He couldn't see her right away; the stacks of crates were in the way. But he knew she was there. He could feel her. No, wait. He stopped walking. Why could he feel her? He hadn't been able to feel her last time. He looked around the room as the hair on the back of his neck came to attention. He wasn't alone, but who was in there with him?

He closed his eyes and listened, feeling for more clues. Someone, at some point, had tied her to that chair. She hadn't done it to herself.

But he didn't get any more clues, so he psyched himself up and started walking again.

And she came into view.

And sure enough, she wasn't alone.

Stephen stopped. "What are you doing here?"

Jeremiah's eyes were wide, not a hint of sleep in them. Had he dreamed from his house?

"I rode my bike," he said quietly.

"You what?"

Her eyes flickered back and forth between them. She was tied to a chair. She probably didn't care how Jeremiah had gotten there.

"Where are you in the house? I mean, you know, the *other* part of the house."

"I was in the chair beside you."

Stephen turned his attention to the girl. "We want to help you. But I don't know how." He felt so helpless. He hated it.

He was waiting for her to come up with an idea? And share it while she was gagged?

She looked at her feet, and his eyes followed hers.

She dragged the toe of her work boot through the thin layer of dust, making a circle. *Brilliant.* He stepped closer as she picked her foot up and began to draw a line beside the circle. He held his breath—a loud smack sounded, and her head jerked sideways, blood flying from her lip.

Stephen jumped back, yanking Jeremiah with him. He hurriedly scanned the area, but there was no one there. Then, in his peripheral vision, a motion, a blur of shadows. His eyes flitted to the corner, but by the time he could focus, there was nothing there.

His eyes returned to the girl, who had fallen still, her head lolled on her shoulder. Her chest rose and fell, but she was unconscious.

CHAPTER 12

"What just happened?" Jeremiah cried.

"We have to get out of here." Stephen reached for Jeremiah's arm, but he yanked it out of reach.

"No! I'm not leaving her."

"Yes, we are." Stephen couldn't see anyone else in that giant room, but something had been there, obviously. She hadn't hit herself.

Was it gone now? He couldn't tell. "It's not safe."

Hadn't Jeremiah seen what he'd seen? Something had struck her. Something had moved so fast that they hadn't seen it. Or worse, it was invisible.

"Come on, we're going." He reached for his arm again, but this time Jeremiah stepped further away.

"You go. I'm not leaving her."

Stephen didn't know what to do. "She's unconscious! She can't tell us anything, and I'm not sure if I want her to, not if it's going to get her ..." Hit? Abused? Killed? He didn't know how to finish the sentence. He was right on the verge of senseless panic.

Jeremiah looked at the lines her foot had drawn in the dust. "O ... L ..." he read.

Stephen shushed him. "Whatever she was trying to write, I don't think we're supposed to know."

Jeremiah scowled. "We *have* to know. I don't know if anyone else knows that she's in here. God sent *us*." His conviction struck Stephen speechless. Who had brought God into this?

Stephen surveyed his surroundings, the ones that could not possibly exist. Bows of ships did not attach themselves to old houses. Shadowy figures did not tie women up for days on end. "Bud," he said quietly, "did you see something, I mean, someone else in here?"

Slowly, Jeremiah shook his head. "I felt it, though. And I don't feel it anymore." And then, while Stephen was still trying to process what he'd just said, he added, "She's been here a long time, I think. She has a *Twilight* tattoo."

Stephen followed Jeremiah's gaze to her upper arm. Sure enough, there was an image of two hands holding a red apple.

She stirred, and they both froze, watching her.

Seconds later, her eyelids fluttered open. Her eyes met Stephen's and then immediately fell to the floor. She picked her foot up to write some more.

"Wait!" Stephen stepped closer. His eyes darted to the corner to his left, which looked so empty. "Maybe you shouldn't. I don't want you to get hurt again."

She shook her head rapidly and started drawing, faster now, and Stephen realized that the second shape hadn't been an L. It had been the top half of a four. She wasn't writing a word. She was writing a number: 04902

She stopped and looked up at him, breathing hard around the rag that gagged her. Just looking at her made him long for a tall glass of water. He couldn't fathom how thirsty she must be.

He walked toward her and then spun around to read the number right side up. He didn't expect this to be much help, but it was. Now he knew exactly what it was: a zip code.

He looked at her. "04902. Where is that?"

Her face fell.

"No, no," he hurried to say, "don't worry. We can figure it out."

She started writing with her foot again, and again, there was a loud slap, and her head careened to the side. Stephen jumped back and then felt guilty. He should have dove toward her to help, but he hadn't. He'd done nothing to protect her. He hadn't even had the instinct to try.

Again, the assaulter was invisible, but this time, she stayed conscious, and fresh tears streamed down her dirty cheeks.

Stephen longed to say something to comfort her, to encourage her, but he didn't know what to say. He looked at the zip code again and reached for his phone. A critical voice screamed at him that he couldn't use a smart phone in la-la land, but he had no idea how else to figure out what town that zip code belonged to. Not in this part of the house, anyway.

He braced himself, expecting some invisible monster to slap the phone out of his hand, but that didn't happen. Jeremiah crept closer to look at the screen as Stephen hurriedly typed the number into the search bar. He pressed the blue search button and held his breath, and then, wonder of wonders, his phone answered his query.

04902 belonged to the town of Mattawooptock, Maine. No wonder she hadn't tried to spell it out. She wouldn't have had enough room. He looked at her and opened his mouth to speak—then changed his mind and snapped it shut. He turned his body to put his back toward the corner. If there was something in that corner, it wouldn't be able to see his face. Then he mouthed. "What about it?"

She looked at him pleadingly.

He didn't understand.

"Do you want us to go there?" Jeremiah asked. "Is there someone there who can help you?"

She nodded and then looked at the corner fearfully.

"We should go," Stephen said. Then he looked her in the eye. "You want us to go? Leave you now and go there?"

Slowly, she nodded. Her eyelids looked like they weighed a ton each.

He started to slide his phone back into his pocket, but then he had an idea. Keeping his body turned, he whispered to her,

"I don't know your name. Can I take your picture, so I have something to show people?"

She nodded readily, and he held his phone up for a quick snapshot, stiffening his whole body in advance of the assault he was sure would come.

No assault happened, and he shoved his phone back into his pocket. "Let's go, Jeremiah."

Jeremiah lingered a moment longer, looking at her, and then followed Stephen to the door and into the hallway.

As soon as Stephen stepped over the threshold, the air around him changed. Cleaner. Lighter. There had been no smoke in the forepeak, but that's what this felt like—stepping out of a smoky room.

A thought occurred to him, and it made his stomach roll with sickness. He looked at the closed door behind them. He did not want to have to go back in there.

CHAPTER 13

"What's the matter?" Jeremiah said.

"Do you think that she meant that we go to Mattawooptock while we're sleeping or while we're awake?" Stephen couldn't believe he'd said the words he'd just said. He was having a complete break with reality.

Jeremiah's eyes were wide. "We can go to a different town while we're asleep?"

"I have no idea. When I offered to go, I assumed she meant ... you know ... in real life."

"What would happen if we woke up, and we weren't ... *here*?"

"That's a good question, and it settles it. Let's try going in real life first. And if that doesn't help, maybe we'll try it ... the other way."

"So when are we going?"

Stephen looked around. "I have no idea. You rode your bike here. Your parents are going to realize that you're gone and panic. We should probably figure out how to wake ourselves up so I can take you home."

"No!" Jeremiah cried.

Stephen shrugged. "I don't know. Maybe they'll give you permission." This wasn't likely. Carrie thought he was a complete nut at best, and at worst, a danger. But did he want to bring a kid to Mattawooptock, anyway? He had no idea what he was going to find there.

Or if he was going to find anything.

Mattawooptock was a small town, but it wasn't *that* small. It had a Walmart. Where was he going to go when he got there? He had no idea. How was he supposed to find the person or thing that was going to know how to help the girl in this house?

He was going to walk around Mattawooptock aimlessly and then give up. This was so crazy and hopeless.

But first, he had to wake up. When he was a kid, he'd always gone back to bed and tried to go back to sleep. But now he needed a faster method, and he didn't have one. "Let's go back to the living room."

"No. The roof."

"The roof? Why?"

"I'll show you." Jeremiah headed up the back stairwell, which was dark as midnight in this version of the house. He'd told Stephen that he avoided these stairs, but now here he was, in the lead.

"Where are we going?" Stephen followed him up the creaking steps, tentatively running his hand along the wall. There was no banister.

"I'll show you," he said again.

Stephen opened his mouth to ask for clarification, and ran his face straight into a net of cobwebs. He gagged and hoping they really were cobwebs and not something worse, quickly swiped them away.

"Are you okay?"

"Not sure. Jeremiah, tell me why the tattoo matters."

"Huh?"

"Why does the tattoo mean that she's been there a long time?"

"*Twilight* is an old movie. No one would get that tattoo nowadays. They'd get made fun of."

"So you think she got it when the movie came out?"

"Yeah. But that was a long time ago. She would have been a little kid."

Stephen wasn't following. "So then either she recently got a tattoo that was popular a decade ago, or she got the tattoo when she little."

"Neither of those things make sense. How could she get a tattoo when she was little?"

The kid had a point.

"She got the tattoo when the movie was popular," Jeremiah said, "and she's been in there ever since."

"What?"

Jeremiah reached the top of the stairs and spun to face him.

In the darkness, Stephen could barely make out his features, but he could feel his frustration.

"We don't know how time works in here. The clocks don't work, and there are fresh flowers in one of the bedrooms."

"What?"

He nodded. "They've been there for a long time, but they don't die."

Maybe they were fake.

"They're not fake."

This was all too confusing. He had to wake up so he could think straight. He looked around. They were in the hallway that led to their bedrooms, but it was wider on this end.

Jeremiah turned and strode confidently away from him, the floorboards creaking beneath his feet. Then he veered right and went into a dark room.

Stephen followed him in and then across the room to a dusty, thick-paned window that Jeremiah wrestled open with a grunt.

He turned and looked at Stephen expectantly. "It's a fire escape."

"What?" Stephen cried. He didn't see any fire escape. He didn't see any anything.

"Yeah. Look." Jeremiah stuck his head out the window and looked down and then up. Then he pulled himself back inside and looked at Stephen triumphantly.

Stephen stepped closer to the window and also stuck his head out. A weathered wooden ladder was nailed flush to the side of the house. He reached out and grabbed the rung below the window. It was wet and slimy. He gave it a shake, and a chunk of it broke off in his hand. He startled and threw it like it was a bloody spider.

He pulled his head inside and looked at Jeremiah. "We cannot put any weight on that. We'll fall. "

"Falling is the whole point." Jeremiah threw one leg out the window, straddling the sill.

Falling was the whole point? What? "No!" Stephen reached for his arm, and again the boy pulled away. He sure was slippery when he wanted to be.

"You do what you want. I know how to wake up. When I do, I'll wake you up too." He swiftly vanished out the window.

Stephen froze. What was he supposed to do now? Whether this was a dream or not, whether this was an alternate dimension or not, he couldn't just let the boy crawl up a rotten ladder. He groaned and gingerly climbed out the window after him. He looked up. Jeremiah was already halfway to the roof. Why on earth did a fire escape need to extend all the way to the roof anyway? Did people hang out up here? Was it also a flood escape? Was there a helipad on the roof? Nothing would surprise him anymore. Maybe the roof was the deck of an aircraft carrier. As he struggled to climb, bits of rotten wood crumbled off in his hands, and the rungs were squishy beneath his tennis shoes.

He didn't see Jeremiah's hand till it was right in front of his face. He grabbed it and let the boy pull him up and onto the asphalt shingled roof. Did Nana's real house have asphalt shingles? Yes, he thought that it did. He looked around. No fighter jets in sight. "Okay." He rubbed his hands together, trying to get the slime and the small bits of wood off. "Now what?"

Jeremiah stepped to the edge and looked down. "Now we jump."

"Now we what?"

"Yeah. Don't worry. This is how I wake up. I always wake up right before I hit the ground."

"Always? How often do you do this?"

He shrugged. "My mom really likes to stay here."

"Okay. Well, I'm not letting you jump off this roof."

Jeremiah gave him a big smile and then took off running.

"No!" Stephen lunged. His fingers brushed against the boy's sweater, but they only brushed. He hurried to look over the edge.

"Jeremiah?" he called, but there was no answer.

He felt completely deflated. Lying on the top of an imaginary roof, looking down into a dark void. What was he supposed to do now?

Someone was shaking his shoulder.

CHAPTER 14

When Stephen saw Jeremiah's face in the dim light, he nearly cried out with relief. He pulled the kid in for a quick hug and then released him just as quickly. "I cannot believe you just jumped off a building."

"It's not a real building."

"Are you sure?"

Jeremiah ignored the question. "The first time, I didn't mean to. I was climbing the ladder, and I slipped, but I woke up before I hit the ground. So the next time I wanted to wake up, I just did it again. Now it's kind of fun."

Stephen shook his head. "We've got to get you out of this house."

"I don't think I'll ever sleep here again. But we have to help her first."

"Fair enough, but I'm not taking you to Mattawooptock."

"You have to!" he cried.

"No. I will go there and see what I can learn, and I promise I'll report back to you. You're a kid, and you're not my kid." It was too bad. He liked him a lot. "I can't just whisk you away in the middle of the night."

"It's not fair! I'm the one who found her!"

Stephen stood up and stretched. He might've slept, but he sure didn't feel rested. "I'll give you a ride home. Let's see if we can wrestle your bike into my trunk."

It wasn't until they reached the light from the streetlamp that Stephen realized Jeremiah was crying. His heart broke for him, but it didn't matter. He was a kid.

The bike did not fit, but it was close enough. Stephen drove slowly across town while the trunk lid bobbed up and down like the head of an old man trying to stay awake in church.

"Something hit her," Jeremiah said thoughtfully, quietly.

"I know."

"What do you think hit her?"

Stephen could feel his gaze. "I don't know."

"I think it was a demon."

Stephen's whole body went cold. "I don't think there's any such thing."

"There is."

Stephen glanced at him. "Why do you think so?" Had he already had some experience with this madness?

"The Bible says so."

Stephen turned his attention back to the road. That wasn't exactly evidence. "Whatever it was, it was a little weird that it didn't try to hit *me*. I was the one offering to help. I'm the one who took her picture." This reminded him that he should check to see if his camera had even worked. Did he actually *have* a picture of her?

"It couldn't hurt me because I have the Holy Spirit inside of me." He looked at him again. "Do you have him inside of you?"

Stephen was too tired for this. He felt guilty for being annoyed with Jeremiah, but he didn't want to further muddle his brain with religious superstitions.

"Do you?" he asked again.

"I don't know."

"Then you don't. You would know if you did."

Stephen didn't say anything.

"We should work on that."

Stephen was glad to pull into Patrick's driveway, but Jeremiah got mad again and didn't say anything else. He only trudged inside, leaving Stephen to unload the bike onto the dark lawn and drive away. He felt bad leaving him behind, but he was also a little annoyed with Jeremiah for not understanding. Would Stephen have understood when he was that age? He thought so. But Stephen had never been in a situation like this when he was that age. He hadn't been in a situation like this in his whole life—till now.

He stopped at an all-night gas station, got a large cup of burnt coffee, and then climbed back into his car and finally checked his camera roll.

His stomach dropped. Yes, he had a photo of her, but *no way* could he show it to anyone. It made him look like a complete madman. She was tied up, bruised, bloodied, and terrified. He'd be arrested instantly and questioned infinitely. And what could he possibly tell them? That he couldn't show them where she was because they couldn't share his dream?

He'd be locked away forever.

He tucked his phone back into his pocket and grudgingly drove to Mattawooptock, desperately trying to come up with a plan.

CHapTer 15

Dawn was breaking when he crossed the Mattawooptock town line, and he doubted anyone would be awake yet save the farmers.

He stopped at the first gas station he came to, put his car in park, and chewed his lip. What was he supposed to do now? He'd been hoping the answer would appear before him like some supernatural message, but there was no such message in sight.

This was just a sleepy Maine town like any other. No evidence of the supernatural in sight.

And then suddenly, the message appeared inside his own head. Whether it was a supernatural download or not he didn't know. Maybe not because it was so obvious that he almost smacked himself in the forehead. He was an artist for crying out loud! He could draw her without the gag! He wasn't a portraitist, but he was no slouch either. He could at least get her main features down on paper.

He turned and looked in the backseat for some supplies, but of course all of his things were still back at the house. Shoot. What time did Walmart open? He was too antsy to sit there for another second to look that up, so he started across town, looking for any store along the way that might be open and might have some paper.

But Walmart *was* open, and gloriously there were few people there. For once he was able to scoot in and out quickly. Then he was back in his car with her photo on his phone and his pencil working furiously. It took a while, and it wasn't perfect, but it was definitely her likeness. He didn't attempt to make her smile, and he left her almost as disheveled as she'd been the last time he'd seen her.

On the next page of the sketchbook, he roughly sketched out her tattoo, which was easier even though he was doing it from memory.

Now he had something to work with. He looked up. He needed to start asking people if they knew who she was. No, that would be too weird. How would he explain that? So he needed to start asking people if they'd seen her.

Good. That could work. But who would he ask?

A woman pulled her minivan up alongside his car. It was weird how closely she parked because the parking lot was nearly empty.

She got out of her vehicle clutching to her chest a small lapdog wearing a pink vest covered in rhinestones. She carried the dog to the cart coral and then placed him in the basket. He was so tiny, it was a wonder he didn't slide out through the cracks.

She started pushing her cart toward the store.

You have to start, or you're never going to start. Stephen took a big breath and pushed himself out of the car. "Excuse me?" He tried to sound non-threatening, but apparently he failed.

She stopped and looked at him suspiciously.

"Sorry to bother you, but have you seen this girl?" He held up the drawing.

Her suspicion visibly grew. "Not interested." She turned and quickly walked away.

"I'm sorry. I didn't mean to startle you. It's important. She's my friend, and I can't find her."

The woman turned and looked. "She's your friend, and you don't have a photo?"

"She doesn't like having her picture taken," he said quickly.

She narrowed her eyes. "Have you tried calling her, or does she not like phone calls either?"

He sighed. He'd been in Tennessee too long. He'd forgotten how decidedly unfriendly New Englanders could be.

"Yes, I have tried calling." Lying was a slippery slope, and he was picking up speed. If he wasn't careful, he was going to lose control and faceplant.

Her expression softened, and she pulled her cart backward, turning for a closer look. "She does look familiar, but I'm sorry,

I can't place her." She looked up at him. "Have you asked the police?"

"Of course."

She pursed her lips as if she knew he was lying and then turned and scurried away. Her dog kept his eyes locked on Stephen's as he rode away. Stephen couldn't be sure, but he thought he saw compassion in those little eyes.

Someone laid on the horn, and Stephen jumped so suddenly that he hurt his back. He spun around, wondering how he could be in someone's way in an empty parking lot. He expected to see some large angry man in a baseball cap with a gun rack ready to beat him up, but what he saw made his stomach sink even more than that would have.

CHAPTER 16

Patrick sat behind the wheel smiling like a fool. Jeremiah sat in the back seat with his face down.

Stephen let out a long sigh and then trudged to Patrick's window, which he rolled down.

"Stevie-boy!" he cried, making Stephen cringe. Then Patrick lowered his voice, "Please don't tell anybody that I'm a part of this. I have a reputation to uphold. But what can I do to help this poor woman?"

Stephen was so shocked that he almost couldn't speak, but he managed, "You believe us?"

"Well I don't know if I believe *you*, but my son doesn't lie to me, so I believe something strange is going on."

Stephen couldn't believe it. He had never tried sharing about his dreams when he was a kid, but he knew without a doubt that if he had shared, no one would have believed him. "How did you find me?"

"Don't all adventures start at Walmart?"

Stephen shook his head slowly. "I don't think so."

Patrick laughed. "Well, if not, then they all stop there along the way. So, what's the plan? How do we find someone who may or may not exist so we can help a woman who may or may not exist?"

That was the most intelligent thing Stephen had ever heard Patrick say. "I don't have a plan. I have no idea what I'm doing."

Patrick pointed his chin at the sketchpad. "What you got there?"

"I tried to draw her." He held up the picture.

Patrick's eyes widened. "Oh my God. That almost looks like... I mean I haven't seen her in years, but that looks like Rosie."

A chill traveled down Stephen's spine. Rosie. He could not know that that was her name, and yet he was confident that it was.

"Does Rosie have a last name?"

"She did. She was Rosie McAllister, but she's probably married by now."

"Any idea why Rosie McAllister would be tied up in an alternate dimension?"

Some color drained from Patrick face. "Man, I hope she's not actually tied up there. I hadn't thought of that." The concern in his eyes was a surprise. "I just assumed it was a dream, you know? Like she's out living her life somewhere, but she's dreaming that she's tied up there? I figured somehow you guys are all sharing the same crazy dream."

"That would be nice, but I don't know why her dream self would send us to Mattawooptock, then."

Patrick nodded. "Good point. Hey, maybe she's in a coma! Maybe she wants us to wake her up!"

Stephen shuddered. That was a creepy thought, and one that he hadn't had.

"Maybe we should go to the hospital, ask if she's a patient there," Patrick said.

It was as good of an idea as any. "Okay, sure."

"Oh, wait! Hang on, I think we're Facebook friends." He whipped out his phone.

"Good idea. If she's posting cat memes, she's probably not in a coma." How and why was Patrick so good at this? Maybe they should have consulted him sooner.

"There she is." He spun the phone around so Stephen could see.

"Do you mind?" Stephen held his hand out.

Patrick readily surrendered the phone.

Stephen zoomed in for a closer look. The resemblance was strong, but this woman looked older than the girl in the fore-peak. He remembered what Jeremiah had said about the tattoo and shuddered. "Could the girl in the house be Rosie's daughter?" Stephen said. People usually used *good* photos, filtered ones even, for their profile pictures. They didn't use ones where they looked older than they really were.

"That could be," Patrick said. "Did you see ..." He pointed his chin at his phone. "It says she lives in Mattawooptock."

Stephen's neck broke out in goosebumps. Some small part of him had still been believing this was all some wacko dream. But it wasn't. Something very real was happening. He scrolled down. "She posted something last night, so there goes the coma theory." That was almost disappointing. He handed the phone back through the window. "Can you message her? Ask her if she has a daughter?"

"No way." Patrick took the phone back. "I haven't talked to her in years. I'm not going to suddenly inquire about her daughter."

"Good point. Can you message her, though? Say something … maybe just ask to talk to her?"

"I suppose." Patrick glanced at the dashboard. "But it's not even seven o'clock yet."

"If you had seen the pain in her eyes, you'd be in more of a hurry." Stephen's gruffness surprised him. He needed to get some sleep, some real sleep. "Sorry, I just mean that whoever is tied up there, if someone really is, she wants us to wake Rosie up."

Patrick wasn't offended—only inexplicably invested in this mission. "Okay. I'll message her."

"Can I come up front, Dad?"

"No, it's not safe. Stay there. Stay buckled up," he said while tapping on his phone screen.

"But the car's not even moving!"

"It will be soon enough." He stopped tapping. "Okay, here's what I've got. Hey, Rosie. I know this is weird, but it's important. I really need to talk to you. Do you have a minute?" He looked up for confirmation.

"I think that works." Stephen didn't have any better ideas.

They both waited. For what, Stephen wasn't sure. Did people respond to social media messages right away? At seven in the morning? He didn't think so. And yet, they waited, not moving, not making a sound.

"Can't you Google her name?" Jeremiah said from the back seat. "Maybe there's an address."

Stephen and Patrick exchanged a look, silently sharing their embarrassment. "Good idea, son. I'll give it a try."

Stephen looked at the sky and then closed his eyes for a moment. He couldn't believe he was on a supernatural mission, but it was even more unbelievable that he was on a supernatural mission with Patrick.

CHAPTER 17

P atrick stopped his car in front of a trash-covered lot in the middle of which sat a dilapidated trailer. There were no cars in the short driveway.

"Well, this doesn't look good," Patrick said.

Across the narrow street a trailer door banged open, and a shirtless man staggered out, tripped on his bottom step, steadied himself, and then stared at the two men and the boy in the car across the street. He squared his shoulders and raised his chin.

"I think we should get out of here," Patrick said.

Stephen didn't know what to do, and he had no argument to give. Even if he had, Patrick wouldn't have listened. He was already executing a not-so-smooth five-point turn in the narrow road. As soon as he got pointed in the right direction, he stomped on the gas.

"What are we doing?" Jeremiah said. "That's her house, right?"

"I don't think that was a safe neighborhood," Patrick said.

Stephen didn't know if any neighborhood in Maine could truly be considered *unsafe*, but it was true that he hadn't felt safe there.

Patrick barely slowed at the end of the street before turning left, and Jeremiah said, "When there's a stop sign, you're supposed to stop and look both ways, Dad."

"You're right, son. Sorry. There's not much traffic here this early. I don't think any of these people have jobs."

Stephen rolled his eyes. "Or they've already left for work."

Patrick looked at him with an eyebrow raised.

"Just because they live in a trailer park doesn't mean they don't work."

Patrick snorted. "You're such a liberal."

"Or I'm just not being a judgmental cretin."

Patrick surprised Stephen with a laugh. "I don't know what that word means, but I doubt it was a compliment." He came to a textbook stop at the second stop sign.

Immediately the back door flew open, and before Stephen knew what had happened, he saw Jeremiah running across the road behind them.

"What the ..." Patrick slammed the car into park and then jumped out and gave chase, leaving the car idling there in the intersection with the driver-side door standing open.

Stephen wanted to chase after the boy as well, but he didn't want to leave the car completely unattended. He got out, went around the hood, and slid behind the wheel. Both Jeremiah and

Patrick were out of sight. It was weird that Jeremiah hadn't run back up the street. Instead, he'd cut across a small field between two houses. Still, Stephen thought he had a pretty good idea where the boy was going, and he turned the car around and headed back toward Rosie's trailer. When he got there, he didn't see either of them. He didn't know what to do. He didn't want to go knock on her door by himself, but if they were already inside ...

He slowly got out of the car and then tentatively crossed the street. He was about to knock on the trailer's front door when he heard voices in the back. Scanning his surroundings for any threats, he tried to look confident as he strode around the trailer toward the voices.

Sure enough, Jeremiah stood on the back steps talking to a woman in the doorway. Patrick stood behind his son with one hand on his shoulder.

"... it's you. I promise." Jeremiah said in a pleading voice. The woman who might be Rosie stared down at him. She was definitely older than the woman in the forepeak. Was she the same person? How was that possible? Of course, if any of this was possible, then that was too. "Have you seen the tattoo?" Stephen asked aloud without really meaning to.

The woman looked up at him.

"On your arm," Jeremiah said quickly, pointing. "A *Twilight* tattoo. Two hands holding an apple."

She narrowed her eyes in skepticism. "Do you know how many people have seen that tattoo? That's not exactly classified information."

"Can we see it?" Stephen asked.

She stared at him, stunned, and then slowly shook her head.

"Please?" Jeremiah pleaded.

"I said no, you freaks!"

"Rosie," Patrick said calmly, gently, "if you show us, and it's not what they're expecting, maybe it makes us all go away."

She surprised Stephen by yanking down on the neck of her shirt. Wouldn't it have been easier to pull her sleeve up?

And there it was. Two hands, holding an apple, except the apple's red had faded to a splotchy orange. And the black lines that made the hands were a dark gray now. It was the same tattoo, but it wasn't. He exchanged a look with Jeremiah. The boy had been right, and he knew it.

This was the same person. She had grown older out here, but not in there. He spoke confidently for the first time in days. "You were wearing a faded black shirt with a large purple butterfly on the front. There was a small hole by the bottom seam."

As his words hit her, the color drained from her face. "What?" She scanned their faces and then took a small step back. "You need to leave. Get off my property."

"I can't," Jeremiah said. "Please. You asked us to come get help. You need help."

Stephen got Patrick's attention to ask, "How much has he told her?"

"The whole thing, I think." Patrick sounded overwhelmed, and he still had a hand on Jeremiah's shoulder. The gesture was a protective one, but Stephen also wondered if he was getting ready to yank his son off the steps and drag him all the way back to the car.

Her eyes landed on Patrick's face. "Do I know you?"

"You used to, yes." Patrick took a deep breath. "We were friends in high school."

Recognition dawned on her face. "*No.* Patrick? Patty-Daddy?" There was a small twinkle in her eyes.

Patty-*what?* What could high school Patrick have possibly done to earn a nickname like that? Stephen glanced at Jeremiah, who looked equally as startled by the moniker.

"Nobody's called me that in a long time, but yeah."

Her emotional reaction was confusing. There was the joy of seeing an old friend, but there was also fear and suspicion. "And what house am I supposedly in?"

"My grandmother's," Patrick said.

She swayed a little and grabbed the door frame. "Nana's house?"

Patrick nodded.

"Okay, enough. I must be trippin'. This isn't possible, but even if it was, what do you expect me to do about it? I can't hop into somebody else's nightmare and rescue myself. Thanks for trying to help, I guess. I think all three of you are insane. You can go now. There's nothing to do here. I'm sorry that you're having nightmares about me."

Stephen stepped closer. "I think you're really there. I don't know how that's possible, but I think you're really there. And you're younger. How long ago did you wear that shirt? And how would I know about it?" He sucked in a breath. "I don't think it's a nightmare."

"I get that *you* think it's real, and I don't know how you know about an old shirt, and maybe you're the one who's trippin'. I don't care. My answer is still go away." She stepped back and started to swing the door shut.

Jeremiah burst into tears, which slowed her down.

"Sorry to bother you, Rosie. If you change your mind..." Stephen hurriedly pulled his wallet out to get a business card.

She took it gingerly and then looked at it closely. She glanced up. "Nashville?"

"Yes, ma'am,"

"You're an artist?"

"He is," Jeremiah said, his voice thick from crying. "He's a wicked good artist. He's famous. You should see the picture he drew of you."

She raised her eyebrows. "You drew me?"

And then suddenly Stephen knew exactly what he needed to do.

CHAPTER 18

"Rosie," Stephen said gently, "I want to show you something, but please don't freak out. It's kind of disturbing."

She grimaced. "You drew a picture of me that is disturbing? Wow, you are a sick freak."

"No, it's not that. The drawing is back in the car. I'll show it to you in a minute if you want. This is something else." He hesitated. He had no idea how she was going to react to this, but she was not going to enjoy it.

She chuckled dryly. "My whole life is disturbing. What is it?"

He pulled his phone out and found her photo. Then he held his breath and held the phone out toward her. He could feel her trepidation, and soon he'd be able to feel her horror.

She took the phone, brought it closer to her face, and then her legs gave out beneath her.

Stephen lunged to catch her and made it in time to soften her landing. Keeping a gentle hand on her arm, he sat beside her on the threshold. "I'm sorry. I know this is scary." He could feel her fear crawling all over him.

"Where am I?" she said, sounding far away. "That doesn't look like Nana's house."

"No it's not her house, but also, it is. I can't explain it," Stephen said.

"That's me." As she studied the picture, grief rolled off her in waves that made Stephen feel ill. "That shirt," she said quietly, talking to herself as she tried to process the unprocessable.

The impossible.

Her eyes lifted to Patrick's. "I knew you."

"You still do, Rosie. I haven't changed that much."

"And you're saying all this is really happening?"

Stephen wasn't sure how Patrick would answer that since he'd never seen the extra rooms in Nana's house, but he nodded gravely. "Yes, this is all really happening."

"You don't remember, do you?"

Patrick furrowed his brow. "Remember what?"

"What happened that night?"

"What night?"

"The night we were at your Nana's house."

"We were only there one night?" He laughed uncomfortably. "I'm sure you came over more than once. Yeah, I remember, you came every time that Maddy and Billy came." It wasn't clear whom Patrick was trying to convince—Rosie or himself.

She shook her head slowly. "I was only there once, and once was enough." Her eyes fell to Jeremiah, who was still crying. "Probably shouldn't talk about that stuff in front of your kid." Her eyes lifted again, and now Stephen thought he saw accusation in them.

Again Patrick laughed uncomfortably. "I don't remember the details, but sure, I'm sure we did some stupid teenage stuff." Was Patrick even aware that he was now inching back from Rosie, his hand slowly sliding off his son's shoulder? Just when he was about to lose his grip, he sank his fingers in, trying to pull Jeremiah back with him, but Jeremiah shook his hand off. For the first time since Stephen had arrived, they weren't touching each other.

"Stupid teenage stuff," she repeated, and her voice sounded like it was coming from far away. "Not exactly what I would call it, but sure ..." A tear fell onto the hand that held his phone.

Stephen wanted to comfort her, but he knew that she didn't want to be touched.

She wiped her nose with the back of one hand as she handed him his phone with the other. "I can't believe you guys came here." She looked at him. "Why on earth did you come here? I mean, I get that some imaginary version of my past self asked for help, but still, you did what she asked? That's insane!"

Stephen didn't think that now was the time to explain that he couldn't ignore the emotional turmoil of another because it was also his emotional turmoil.

"We couldn't not help," Jeremiah said around his tears.

Oh, maybe Jeremiah was going to explain it.

She laughed bitterly. "Oh, I get it. You just want the nightmares to stop."

Jeremiah quickly retorted, "Don't you?"

The sharp edge of his question ticked her off, and she stood abruptly. "Okay, so it's all real. Whatever. It's all some supernatural real-life nightmare. Fine. But it doesn't matter because there's nothing we can do about it. You guys need to go back to where you–"

Stephen reached up and gently took her hand. "Patrick, would you mind taking Jeremiah for a quick walk?"

"What?" Jeremiah cried. "Why? What are you going to do?"

"I just want to ask Rosie something. Please, one minute."

Patrick looked relieved, and he ushered Jeremiah away against his will. As soon as they were out of earshot, Stephen said, "Tell me what happened to you that night."

She stared down at him, her lips quivering. He wanted her to sit back down, but she didn't want to, so he stood and faced her. "It's okay. Tell me."

Sirens sounded in the distance. A fitting soundtrack.

Rosie sniffed again and let out another bitter laugh. Then she looked down at her arm as she slid her sleeve up and showed him the inside of her elbow.

He managed to not gasp. But he didn't know what to say.

The middle of her arm was covered in pale pink scars, new scabs, and deep, purple bruises that reminded him of the color of the butterfly on her shirt. He'd never seen that many track marks on anyone. His eyes flicked up to meet hers. She was lucky to be alive.

"That night was the first time." She yanked her sleeve down and looked up, already regretting having shown him. "So it doesn't make sense, and it does. I guess I'm like trapped there because I'm trapped. That's where I first got trapped." She shook her head in frustration and roughly ran both hands down over her face. "Please, just go. There's nothing you can do for me. Whatever this is, I guess I deserve it. I'll probably die soon, and then your dreams might stop."

His dreams would stop the second he left that house for good. But that wasn't the point. "I don't know what we're supposed to do," he said evenly. "But I do know that you asked for help. Please, let us help you. Is rehab an option?"

She laughed bitterly. "I can't afford rehab. Are you insane?" She looked him up and down in disgust. "Guess rich fancy artists in the city just go to rehab whenever they want."

He worked at not being annoyed by her judgment. "There's got to be an option. What about the ER? They could give you a Suboxone prescript—"

She laughed again. "I'm not going back on subs."

"You've tried it before?"

"I was on it for months. Stopped taking it. Then back on it for months again. And then ... It won't work. Just trust me." She was getting antsy. She wanted to go back inside, be done with them.

The sirens grew louder.

Patrick was looking at him, and Stephen nodded that they could come back. Maybe Patrick would have an idea.

"She's uh …" Stephen said to Patrick. He pointed to the crook of her arm. "She has a horse problem."

She rolled her eyes. "Oh come on. He's not that little. He goes to school, right?"

But Jeremiah's sheltered innocence was written all over his face. And then, just in case she missed it, Jeremiah said, with a healthy dose of defiance, "I don't go to school. I'm home-schooled."

"Whatever." She let out a jagged sigh and turned to go inside, but then her whole body jerked. "Did you hear that?"

"What?" Patrick said.

They all froze, listening.

"The sirens?" Patrick asked.

She looked at Stephen, her eyes wild. "Where's your car?"

"Out front."

Rosie took off running.

CHAPTER 19

Stephen gave Patrick a bewildered look and then took off after Rosie.

"You want to help?" she cried out in complete panic. "This is how!"

He'd almost caught up to her when she stopped suddenly, spun around, and came right back toward him, her arms flailing, her messy hair flying out wildly behind her. "It's too late!"

He didn't know what to do, so he simply watched her run by him and then turned to watch her run by Patrick and Jeremiah too. She headed straight for the back yard of the trailer behind hers.

Patrick said, "If you want to try to follow her, we can get the car and catch up to you. Or we can just go home."

Stephen knew he was hoping to be assigned the latter task.

"I'll try to follow. I'll text you where I end up." He started after her. He moved quickly, but he didn't need to run because her path was not a straight line.

"Where are you going?" he called out, but she gave no indication that she heard him.

He hoped she wasn't going someplace scarier than the one she'd fled.

She crossed a street without so much as looking for traffic and then did the same thing at the next street. He grew tired as they grew closer to downtown Mattawooptock.

Suddenly she turned and started running straight up busy Route 201, making a complete spectacle of herself.

He slowed down, not wanting to be part of the show. She'd chosen to run uphill, so she soon slowed as well, and then she was ducking behind a gas station.

He hurried, a little nervous that she was out of sight.

He needn't have worried.

She sat behind the station, her head between her knees, panting. She looked up when he approached. "I can't believe you're still here. I don't suppose you have a cigarette?" She laughed, which led to a fit of coughing.

"No, I sure don't." He scooched beside her, not wanting to sit on the dirty asphalt. "Why are you afraid of the cops?"

"I didn't show up for court. I don't think they're after me. I think they're after my boyfriend, but I have warrants, so they would've scooped me up."

He could feel her fear, but it seemed excessive. But he knew that fear had a way of doing that. So often fear stretched beyond logic, filling the space where reason used to live, and sucking all the air out of that space.

She gave him a look. "Have you ever gone through withdrawals in a jail cell? Well, I have. I thought it would kill me, and then I wished it would."

"So where are you going to go?" He took out his phone.

"Who are you calling?" she snapped, paranoid.

"Patrick. Once you tell me where we're going, I thought maybe we could get a ride there."

She shook her head. "I don't know where to go. I'll just wait it out and then go home." She looked around quickly, reminding Stephen of a scared rabbit.

"Where is your boyfriend?"

"I don't know." She stood up suddenly. "I'm gonna go. You go home. I'll be okay." She struggled to get herself back onto her feet and then she started walking.

He considered letting her go. He was beyond tired. But stubbornness pushed him to follow. He texted as he walked, telling Patrick where he was.

A minute later, Patrick pulled his car alongside them as she cut across a laundromat parking lot that was mostly potholes.

He threw the car into park so quickly that the whole car jerked forward and back. Jeremiah jumped out. Patrick turned the engine off and then was right behind him. "Why did you run?" he cried accusingly.

She ignored him.

He looked to Stephen for help, but Stephen had no help to offer.

"There!" Jeremiah pointed up the road.

They all turned to look.

"What?" Patrick said. "What do you see?"

"It's a church."

"So?" Rosie said.

"Sorry, his mother has been taking him to church every week. The kid is beyond brainwashed."

"Sorry to disappoint you," Rosie said, "but that's a homeless shelter."

Jeremiah started walking. "But it's got a steeple."

It did look like a church. Without really thinking about it, Stephen followed Jeremiah.

"What are you two doing?" Patrick cried out.

Stephen didn't know. He was just following his friend, following his confidence.

Jeremiah turned and looked at his father like he was a moron. "It's a church, Dad. We need help. That's what churches do. That's their job. They help people." He turned and started walking again.

"Son, you have no idea what you're talking about. Churches don't …" He stopped talking because his son was ignoring him. And he was almost out of earshot.

Stephen turned back to look at Rosie, who wasn't yet following. He stopped walking, torn. He wanted to support Jeremiah, but he didn't want to lose Rosie. "Hey, Jeremiah, hold up a sec." He tried to keep his tone light, so Jeremiah didn't think he was criticizing him. "I think Rosie needs a bit of convincing."

"It's a homeless shelter," Rosie repeated. "I'm not homeless!" Somewhere deep down, she still had some pride, and it was slowing her down.

Jeremiah stomped back toward them, his face pinched. "You might not know it, but you are tied to a chair, and you can't do anything!" His voice was wild. "You are bleeding. You are cold and hungry and tired. And you can't move. You can't leave. You can't even stand up. Now come with me, please! You're the one who asked us to help you!"

Patrick's mouth hung open.

Rosie didn't look convinced yet, but Patrick now did. "Son, it's a Saturday," Patrick said gently. "I doubt it's even open."

"Someone's there," Rosie said quietly. "Someone's always there."

"Come on, let's go." Jeremiah waved his hand over his head and then turned and started walking again. And the three adults followed. Stephen couldn't believe it, but they followed, leaving the car behind.

CHAPTER 20

As Stephen drew closer to the homeless shelter, he could read the sign: Open Door Church. So they were both right. This didn't shock him. He knew of a few churches in Nashville who were doing something similar.

But he didn't know if this church-shelter would be able or willing to help Rosie. He admired Jeremiah's childlike faith, but it might be naive. He hoped Jeremiah wouldn't be too hurt and disappointed. How many blows could a childlike faith endure before it evaporated?

And Rosie didn't even want to get well, and she was being forced through their doors by this ridiculous trio, two members of which hadn't slept in a long time and practiced supernatural dream travel.

Stephen sped up, trying to beat Jeremiah to the church, but the boy was the first one to open the door. Stephen caught it before it could swing shut and held it open for Rosie, whose feet were dragging, and Patrick who was bringing up the rear like a herd dog.

As the door swung shut behind them, a giant man asked, "Can I help you?" He towered over them, nearly as wide as he was tall.

Jeremiah pointed his thumb over his shoulder. "My friend Rosie needs help. The grownups won't tell me what's wrong with her, but I think it's a God thing."

The man was beyond confused. Who could blame him? He hesitated and then said, "Hang on. I'll go get the pastor. He's in charge."

The lobby was brightly lit, clean, and smelled like lemons. Not exactly what Stephen had expected.

"We should go," Rosie said. "This is so stupid. I'm not homeless."

"Go where?" Patrick asked.

"I don't know. That guy wanted to take me to the E.R. Let's go there." She shifted her weight from foot to foot.

"E.R.?" a man said as he approached. He was also tall, though not nearly as tall as his greeter had been. His smile was sincere, and his eyes had laugh lines. Bits of silver flecked his dark hair. He wore a Skillet T-shirt and faded blue jeans with paint on them. If this was the pastor, he sure didn't look like one. "Is someone sick?"

Stephen opened his mouth to answer, but Jeremiah beat him to it. "Tell him what's wrong. I won't listen." He stuck his fingers into his ears and started to sing.

Just when Stephen thought this scene couldn't get more preposterous, now the kid was loudly singing a catchy tune about roaring like a lion.

The pastor's smile widened. He looked at Stephen. "I like him. Is he your son?"

"No, he's mine," Patrick said quickly.

His eyes slid to meet Patrick's. "Well, good job, Dad. I have two of my own. I know it can be tricky." He looked at Rosie. "What's up?" He stepped closer, and she shrank back against the wall.

"We should go." She edged toward the door.

The pastor in painted jeans watched her for a few seconds and then looked at Stephen. "Would you guys like to sit down?"

Stephen nodded quickly.

"Right this way. He led them a short distance down the hall and then through two large doors and into the sanctuary, which was spacious. A few people milled around up front, but they ignored the newcomers.

He pointed to the back row. "Make yourself comfortable."

Rosie fell into a chair, hugging herself. Stephen tried to convince himself that she was just emotionally overwhelmed, but he could feel her chemical hunger.

The pastor sat in the chair in front of her, turning his body so he could easily see her, and then extended his hand. Reluctantly, she shook it. "Hi. I'm Galen. How can I help you?"

She didn't answer.

"Someone has to tell him," Jeremiah said after a second. "I can't because you won't tell me."

"She's battling an addiction," Stephen said. "We're trying to convince her to let us help her."

He didn't even blink. This wasn't strange at all. Not yet, anyway.

"Okay. Yeah, we can definitely help with that. Are you family?"

Rosie snickered. "Hardly. I don't even know them."

Now Galen's expression flickered. "Okay."

"I used to know her," Patrick said. "We were friends in high school."

Galen looked relieved. So they hadn't just dragged some stranger in off the street.

Rosie's knee bounced up and down.

Gradually, subconsciously, the rest of them drifted closer to Rosie until she was almost surrounded. Patrick stood awkwardly beside her, and the two dreamers stood behind. If she wanted to make a run for it, she would have to go to her right. It was the only option. But then she'd have to get by the two dreamers before she could reach the door.

Essentially, they had her penned in.

"What's your name?" Galen asked.

"Rosie."

"Hi, Rosie. I'm sure this is all pretty alarming, but please hear me when I say that many people have been where you are and are in much better spots now. What are you addicted to?"

"Heroin," she said matter-of-factly.

Galen did not react at all. Neither did Jeremiah. Maybe he knew more than he had let on. "Okay, anything else?" Galen asked.

She shrugged. "My vape."

He nodded. "Okay. Do you have a Suboxone prescription?"

She shook her head. "I used to, but not for a long time."

"Okay. And do you want to quit?"

She didn't answer him.

"Do you want to get clean?"

Still no answer.

"Because we could try to force you, but it won't do much good unless this is what you want."

Quickly, Stephen went to the other end of her row, not because he wanted to block her escape but because he was worried she'd forget about how much support she had. He wanted her to be able to see him.

He sat down beside her. "Please, Rosie. You can do this."

"Yes," Galen agreed. "You can. But you have to decide to."

She shook her head. "I can't."

Stephen felt Galen give up. He only leaned back an inch, and his facial expression didn't change, but still, Stephen felt it.

Jeremiah must have felt it too because he blurted out, "She's tied to a chair!"

CHAPTER 21

Galen looked up at Jeremiah. "She's tied to a chair?"

Oh boy. How were they going to explain *that*?

"She's tied to a chair in a different house, and she asked us ..." He started crying at the beginning of his sentence, and the tears wouldn't let him finish.

Galen looked to Stephen for clarification.

Stephen took a breath. He couldn't leave his little protégé hanging, but he also didn't want to start sputtering supernatural nonsense to a man of the cloth. Even if this man of the cloth was in paint-covered jeans.

"You know, I've been at this a while. I've pretty much heard it all."

Stephen swallowed. He'd be willing to bet the man hadn't heard *this*. "It's hard to explain."

Galen looked the boy dead in the eye. "Son, did you have a vision?"

Slowly, Jeremiah shook his head.

"Something like that," Stephen said. "It was a dream."

"It wasn't a dream!" Jeremiah snapped. "It was real."

Somehow, Galen didn't look fazed.

"And I've had it too," Stephen said.

Galen's eyes widened a little. "Now, that *is* interesting."

"When I sleep in Nana's house," Jeremiah said, his voice shaking, "I wake up, and the house has extra rooms. I was exploring them when I found—"

"Stop!" Patrick said firmly.

Jeremiah's lip quivered. He had to be so tired.

Galen smiled at Patrick. "Sir, remind me later to tell you about the time I was shot in the chest and only suffered a hole in my t-shirt. I've been exposed to the supernatural. But for now, can you let your son explain?"

Patrick's eyes widened in wonder, and he nodded.

Galen looked at Jeremiah, but he didn't say anything.

"I've been having the dream since I was a kid," Stephen said. "I've had it more times than I can count, actually. Always the same rooms. Used to scare the tar out of me, but Jeremiah is braver than I was and did more exploring, and he's the one who found Rosie, in one of those extra rooms, gagged and tied to a chair." He didn't think he needed to mention that the particular room Rosie was in was part of a ship. This was crazy enough without the details. "I didn't know that he was having the dreams too," he hurried to add. "Until I saw him in there. Or rather, he saw me."

"You're having the same dream, together? At the same time?"

"It's not a dream," Jeremiah mumbled.

Galen nodded quickly. "I understand. Just not sure what else to call it yet. Don't worry, I believe you."

How or why he believed them Stephen couldn't imagine. Unless that bullet in the chest thing was true.

Galen looked at Rosie. "And you have the dream too?"

She shook her head. "No," she said softly, "but that's the house I was in the first time I used."

Galen exhaled and sat up straighter. "Oh. Wow."

"In the dream," Stephen said, "or whatever it is, she asked us to help her. She asked us to come to Mattawooptock."

His eyes widened, and he focused on Rosie. "But you don't know about this? You don't know that you asked for help?"

She shook her head.

Galen looked her over quickly and said, "Okay, I'll admit, I don't understand most of this, so let's focus on what I do understand. We've got an active addiction, and you haven't used in a while, correct?"

She nodded.

"Okay, so we need to move. Did we learn anything else from that other version of Rosie that could help us?" he asked Stephen.

Stephen forced himself to concentrate. "Not that I can think of."

"Okay. If you think of anything, don't be afraid to pipe up." He looked at Jeremiah. "That goes for you too. But for now, Rosie, you have to decide right now because you know what's happening to you right this second. Do you have any drugs on you?"

She shook her head.

"Okay, so then you're either about to bolt to the door or let us help you. Which is it?"

She couldn't decide.

For the first time, Galen showed impatience. "It's up to you."

"Okay." She whimpered.

"Okay, we're quitting?"

She nodded. "Okay."

"Okay, good. Let's get you to urgent care and get you a prescription. Then we'll bring you back here if you want. I'll make some calls. There are some faith-based rehab-like programs that might have a spot for you. I don't know what I can find on a Saturday, but I'll try."

She didn't try to hide her skepticism.

"We can get you there, but it will be up to you to stay there and do the work. Until then, you can stay here. We've got an empty room that you can have for now so that you can have some privacy." Galen stood. "If you've got loved ones who will worry, please let them know that you're okay, and please *don't* tell them where you are." His jaw grew firm as he looked down on her. "Do you have a boyfriend?"

She nodded.

"And he uses?"

She kept nodding.

"Don't tell him either. You know why?"

She just stared at him, but yes, she knew why.

"Why?" Jeremiah asked.

Galen gave him a long look, measuring him. "That chair she's tied to? I think that the chair is the addiction. It's like a prison cell. And if she tries to get free, the other people in her life won't like that. They want her to stay trapped in there with them. So we need to protect her from people who are going to want to add more ropes to that chair. Does that make sense?"

The terror in Jeremiah's eyes made it clear that he understood perfectly.

"Okay, we don't all have to go, but Rosie does. Let's go get in my truck."

She didn't move.

"I'm not going to force you, Rosie. And it seems these three gentlemen have already worked hard enough to get you this far. The rest is on you." He gave her a few seconds. "But Rosie? I mentioned that I've seen people get free of this? I've also seen people not get free, and I'm telling you that this might be your last chance. Some of those people are dead now." He said it so matter-of-factly. He wasn't being cold, exactly, but he sure wasn't being warm and fuzzy.

But it worked. She stood up and with shaky legs, followed him toward the door.

Patrick motioned to Stephen to slow down. "Looks like we did it. I'm going to take Jeremiah home now, let him get some sleep."

"No!" Jeremiah cried.

Stephen didn't want to side with Patrick over Jeremiah, but Patrick was right this time. "I'm pretty sure the excitement is over," he said to Jeremiah. "I promise I will report back to you if anything changes." He looked at his first cousin. "Is that all right with you?"

"Oh yeah," Patrick said quickly. "Please do."

Stephen squeezed Jeremiah's shoulder and then hurried after Rosie and the pastor.

He'd almost missed his ride.

Galen was backing out of his parking spot when he saw Stephen approaching. He rolled down the window. "You want to come along?"

Stephen nodded and jumped in the back seat. "Thanks. I might not be needed, but I'd like to see this thing through."

"Grateful to have you. I just tried to get my wife to come, but she's not answering her phone." He was not worried about this, though. That was clear.

If Stephen were married to someone with a job like this, he'd dodge phone calls too.

CHAPTER 22

The urgent care lobby was empty, and Galen marched confidently up to the counter. When a woman in bright pink scrubs appeared, he said, "Good morning, Amy."

"Good morning, G. What's up?" Through the scratched safety glass, she looked Stephen and then Rosie up and down. The gold cross pendant on her chest was noticeably large and matched the gold crosses hanging from her earlobes.

"This is Rosie. She's about to go into active withdrawal. I was hoping to get her a script."

"Oh sure, come on in." She waved them toward a closed door, but Stephen took a seat in the waiting room. He watched them go, shook his head in wonder, and then took out his phone. It was nearly dead, so he looked around the room for some magazines instead. He didn't spend a lot of time in medical waiting rooms, but he was sure it had been a decade since he'd picked up a magazine in one.

He'd read a two-year-old *People* magazine and was halfway through a newer *Town & Country* when they came back into the waiting room.

Rosie didn't look so good.

They visited the checkout window and then Galen smiled at him on his way by. Stephen jumped up and followed them to the truck.

"Thank you," Rosie said when Galen started the truck.

"It's my pleasure." He looked at her. "Truly."

"I don't know how this is going to be any different than the last time, but ..."

"It's different."

Why was he so confident? He'd prayed for her, quite passionately, on the way to the clinic. Was that what he thought her last attempt had been missing—God? Prayer? Or maybe she had a better support network this time. Or maybe he was confident he'd be able to get her into a facility with a high success rate. Stephen didn't know where Galen got his confidence, and he was envious of it.

Galen's eyes found Stephen's in the rearview. "So you've had multiple dreams, and each time the layout of the rooms is the same?"

"Yeah."

"Wow. That's crazy."

What was crazy was that this guy believed any of this so readily. Of course, he claimed he'd had a bullet supernaturally removed. No way was that true. Maybe the nice pastor was a wing nut.

"And is the layout of rooms the same in every building you have the dream in?"

"Oh, it only happens in my grandmother's house."

"Really? Wow! Isn't that strange!"

This was the part that shocked him?

"And have you ever run into anyone else in any of these rooms?"

Stephen thought of the shadow in the corner. "No, no one else. I thought it was just my recurring nightmare. I would still think that if Jeremiah hadn't told me he'd seen me in there."

"Nightmare? What made the dream so scary?"

"I was just a kid," Stephen said, feeling defensive. "Some parts of the house look scary. Old, cobwebs, rotten wood. Disconcerting details that felt disturbing ..."

"Ah, yes. It makes sense that there would be chaos there."

It did? "And it just felt so real—"

"It was real." Galen glanced at him again. "Sorry, didn't mean to interrupt. And don't mean to be too nosy either. It's just all so fascinating."

"Maybe."

"Maybe? You don't think it's awesome how God orchestrates impossible things to save people?" He turned to Rosie. "He must have big plans for you."

She snorted.

"Okay, we'll talk about that later." He tightened his grip on the steering wheel. "One step at a time." He glanced at the rearview again. "So you're welcome to hang out as long as you want, or I can find you a ride somewhere."

Stephen didn't know the answer to that. He didn't trust Rosie to stay the course, but what could he do here?

"Stay," Rosie said weakly. "I mean, if you can."

"I can," he said quickly. Thank goodness for bereavement leave.

"Where do you live?" Galen asked after a quiet moment.

"Nashville."

"That's so cool. Never been."

"It's a good place to visit."

"Yeah. Maybe I will when I retire."

Stephen had doubts that this man would ever retire.

Galen pulled into a drugstore parking lot. He looked at Rosie. "You want me to run in?"

She nodded.

"Thank you," she said softly when Galen had shut the door. "I don't understand any of this. And I'm about to get pretty mean, I think. So before that happens, I should thank you."

"You're welcome." He couldn't quite muster up a "it's my pleasure" as the pastor had done, but he wasn't a pastor.

He'd make a pretty bad pastor with his lack of faith.

Though, given everything he'd experienced in the last few days, maybe there was a God. Or at least a good power. There was certainly an evil power, so there had to be a good one to balance that out, right? Otherwise the whole world would look like that creepy extra hallway on the second floor of his Nana's house.

Galen climbed back into the truck and handed her a large paper bag.

"I don't have any money."

"Don't worry about that. We have a slush fund for moments such as these. "

She chuckled dryly. "You even paid the nickel."

Galen laughed. "That I did."

Stephen waited for an explanation, didn't get one, and felt left out. "The nickel?" What could one possibly get for a nickel?

Galen laughed again. "Yeah, in Maine they charge you a nickel per bag. It's illegal to give us plastic, and they have to charge us for the paper."

Oh. So *that* was why the mean clerk in Jay had forced the paper bag on him. "They've tried to do that in Nashville before. I didn't realize anyone had actually pulled it off."

"I think I'm going to be sick." She reached for the door handle, and Galen yanked the truck onto the shoulder.

She got the door open just in time and didn't bother getting out.

Not much came up. She hadn't eaten in a while, which was probably a good thing.

Galen waited patiently until she pulled herself back in and shut the door. "Go ahead and take a sub. It'll help."

"If the taste doesn't make me throw up again."

She didn't have anything left to throw up.

"I got you some lemon drops too. They're in there, but wait to eat one. You know the deal."

"Yeah, I know the deal." She pawed at the bag.

Stephen didn't know the deal, but he was glad they'd stumbled onto a pastor who somehow knew all about this stuff.

"Want me to get one out for you?" Galen asked.

"No, I got it." She was struggling, though. Her hands were shaking, and she was breathing hard. But she got the box open and then started battling one of the packets. Her hands not cooperating, she gave up and handed it to Galen, who opened it and gave her the small tab of medication, which she hastily put in her mouth. Then she pressed her body back into the seat and exhaled.

Galen started the truck and pointed them toward the church.

CHAPTER 23

Stephen met Galen's wife soon after getting Rosie moved into her room. Maggie was lovely, treating Rosie like an honored guest instead of a junkie nuisance. Rosie took to her immediately.

Stephen was stunned by how well the medicine was working. Rosie wasn't happy by any stretch, but her physical symptoms seemed to be cured—for the moment at least. She stared out the window, though the view of the parking lot was not that impressive. "Dwight has got to be freaking out." It wasn't clear who she was talking to. Maybe no one.

Maggie looked at him, silently asking who Dwight was.

"Boyfriend?" Stephen guessed.

Rosie nodded without looking at them but then spun around. "Yeah. I live with him. Anyway, he's going to be looking for me. He's going to be really mad. He needs me to help him with ... stuff."

Maggie stepped closer to her. "Hear me when I say this. You *cannot* be worried about him right now. This is life or death, and it's your life or death, not his. You want to worry about him? That path leads to death."

Whoa, she was taking off the gloves.

"No one knows you're here. You've got your own bathroom so that it stays that way. This is your chance."

"There was a big guy when we first came in," Stephen said. "Does he know anything about her?"

"Tiny? It's okay. He doesn't live here anymore. He was just visiting, and he's already gone."

"Are you sure we're talking about the same guy?" That man had been anything but tiny.

Maggie smiled. "The name is ironic."

"So you don't think he'll find me?" Rosie was feeling a weird mix of guilt and fear and was annoyed that Stephen had distracted Maggie by questioning some stranger's nickname.

"I don't know," Maggie said. "I don't know him. I do know that he will have a hard time getting past Galen. I can also tell you that there's absolutely no way he will take you by force. But we won't do that either. This isn't a jail cell. You stay here for as long as you want or until Galen finds you a spot somewhere better. But if you decide to leave, we'll let you. So ..." She took a big breath. "Like I said, he is the least of your worries. You need to worry about yourself. Okay? Don't be so busy worrying about his sabotaging you that you sabotage yourself."

Rosie nodded soberly. She wasn't comforted.

Maggie turned to Stephen. "You want some lunch?"

What he really wanted was a nap, but he wasn't sure he could request a bed at a homeless shelter. And he wasn't sure he'd want to if he could. "Sure. Thanks."

"Follow me. We'll bring you back something, Rosie."

"I'm not hungry."

"I know." Maggie closed the door behind them.

"She's in pretty good shape," Stephen said. "I was expecting much worse."

"If she keeps taking the medication, she'll be okay physically. We need to worry about her spiritual health."

Stephen was glad Maggie couldn't see his face because he didn't know if he could mask his skepticism. He now had to admit that there were things in the world that he didn't understand, but all this Jesus stuff was giving him a headache.

The large basement cafeteria was a busy place, and Stephen regretted his visit. He felt guilty eating the homeless people's food. But Maggie was there too, filling up her plate, so he fell in line.

They sat at a long skinny table, and she introduced him to a few nearby people. He tried to be pleasant, but he was uncomfortable.

And Maggie knew it. "Are you doing okay?" She took a bite of her sandwich.

"Yeah, yeah." He tried to be convincing.

She smiled as she chewed, and her eyes twinkled. She swallowed. "I know, it's a lot. You get used to it, though."

And that was part of what was bothering him. He didn't want to be this uncomfortable. It made him feel like a jerk. And he shouldn't be this uncomfortable. He wasn't a naive, sheltered person. "I live in Nashville. We have lots of people there who are unhoused."

She nodded thoughtfully. "I've heard that."

He sighed, trying to ignore the weight on his shoulders, which reminded him why he didn't like being around people with nowhere to go. He could feel their hopelessness like a heavy blanket. He tried to think of a silver lining. "Our churches are helping, though. I know of a few that have done what you do here." He looked around. "Though I don't think they have as much room."

She smiled. "We had an addition put on."

That made sense. He wondered how they could have a room open for Rosie—one with a private bathroom no less.

"What does your church do for them?" She said it conversationally, without a hint of judgment. She was genuinely curious, but he still felt ashamed.

"Uh, I don't really have a church."

"No? Why not?" Still, no judgment. "I'm a little jealous. Must be so many vibrant churches in your area."

He leaned back. He was too tired to eat any more. He was also too tired to be having this conversation. "I'm just not much for organized religion, I guess."

"I can understand that. But can I offer you some free advice?"

He forced a smile. "Sure."

"Make sure that while you're avoiding organized religion, you don't accidentally avoid Jesus." She took another bite of her sandwich, and Stephen busied himself with his cup of tepid lemonade. It tasted like the diet powdered stuff his grandmother used to make him, but it was better than continuing this conversation.

CHAPTER 24

"Great news!" Galen met Stephen and Maggie at the top of the stairs.

"You did it," Maggie said.

"God did it."

Maggie rolled her eyes and looked at Stephen. "He never takes any credit." She put her hands on her hips and looked at her husband. "God did not pick up the phone and dial those numbers. You did."

"Let's not fight in front of the guests, honey. Anyway, His Mansion has a spot for her."

"Awesome! When?"

"As soon as we can get her there."

"His Mansion?" Stephen said. Sounded like more Jesus balderdash.

"It's a fantastic residential treatment program in New Hampshire," Maggie said. "They'll take good care of her."

Several emotions hit Stephen at once: fear, doubt, joy, and disappointment. "That's it? We just ship her off?"

Maggie gave him an understanding smile. "They allow visitors. But yes. She needs to get away from the people she's been with." Maggie rubbed his arm. "I know it's hard, but this is a good thing."

Stephen was embarrassed. He had no reason to be feeling so attached to her. "I haven't even known her twenty-four hours. It's okay."

Galen raised his eyebrows. "You met her before today, though, didn't you?"

Stephen nodded and looked at the floor, trying to pretend a lump wasn't forming in his throat. Yes, in a way, he had.

"Attachment forms pretty quickly when we're in crisis. I've got to go to a meeting in a little bit, but I'm going to have one of our deacons and his wife drive her down. I'm sure they won't mind if you want to ride along?"

"It's okay. I have to get back to work." He had to get back to his life. "But thank you." He forced himself to pick his head up. "I would like to say goodbye, though."

"Of course. Let's go. You can even tell her the good news if you want."

"No, thank you. I'll let you do it."

Stephen was nearly certain that Rosie wouldn't still be in her room. She'd have climbed out the window or something.

But she opened the door when Galen knocked. Her eyes fell to the food. "I'm really not hungry."

"I know," Maggie said again. "But I'll just leave this. Try to pick at it if you can. And if you don't, that's okay too." She set the tray on the small desk. It barely fit.

Galen cleared his throat. "So it turns out I was right."

Rosie stared at him expectantly.

"God does have big plans for you. I thought it might take weeks to find you a spot somewhere, but there's a nice facility in New Hampshire that can take you right away."

"A rehab?"

"Sort of. It's a ministry. So they're going to tackle your addiction from a spiritual angle, but don't worry, they're trained. They know what they're doing."

She still looked skeptical. "And they'll take me?

Galen nodded. "I have a friend there. They'll take you."

Her eyes traveled from face to face and back to Galen's. "But why would you vouch for me? How do you know I won't just run away?"

If she was thinking thoughts like that, maybe it was a good idea she was moving to a different state.

"I don't know that. But I do know that God has gone to pretty great lengths to get you this far, and I'm confident he'll get you the rest of the way."

She stood there for a long time, frozen in place. Galen and Maggie watched her process with a patience Stephen did not share.

Finally, she said, "Okay. I'll do it. But they're not like weirdos, right?"

Galen frowned. "Weirdos?"

"They're not going to like, try to *religion* the drugs out of me." She made air quotes around the word *religion*.

Maggie laughed. "That might be the first time I've heard the word used as a verb, and yet I know exactly what you mean. I don't think they're going to thump it out of you with a Bible, no."

"They're not going to hit me at all, right?"

"Good grief, girl, what TV shows have you been watching?" Maggie said.

She hesitated. "Uh, all of them?"

Maggie shook her head. "No. No follower of Jesus is going to strike you, ever." She started toward the door as she talked and then stopped. "Unless it's self-defense. I mean, you're not going to take a swing at them, right?"

Rosie actually laughed. Really laughed. "No. I don't plan to."

Maggie nodded. "Okay good. Then there should be no violence."

The moment was surreal. There was actual palpable joy in the room.

Rosie's eyes fell on him, and Galen and Maggie slipped out of the room.

"I'd like to keep in touch," he said, "if you wouldn't mind."

"Actually, I was going to ask you for your number."

Oh good. He'd felt like he was going out on a shaky limb there.

"I was wondering if you would do me one more favor," she said.

"Sure." He stepped closer.

"I know it's a big ask, but I was hoping you might go take one more nap in that house?" She chuckled uncomfortably.

"Oh yeah. Don't worry. I was going to do that anyway." She wasn't the only one who had to know.

"Yeah?" Her eyes widened. "And you'll go to the room I'm in? Or I was in? I'm hoping that I'm not still there. Or that I get out of there soon."

"Yeah, I'll go."

She nodded. "Okay. Um, boy, I don't know how to say this, but don't lie to me okay? If I'm still there, please tell me. I need to know."

He nodded. "I won't lie to you."

"Thank you. I don't know how to thank you, but thank you. I know you could have just left and not come after me."

He'd wanted to. Jeremiah wouldn't let him. But he was reluctant to admit that to her. "It was Jeremiah's idea too."

She smiled. "What a weird kid. Would you thank him too for me?"

"I will."

She nodded and crossed the room. She wrapped her arms around him, and he returned the embrace, stunned by how thin she was. Her frailty reminded him of Nana the last time he'd hugged her. He carefully let go of her.

"You gave me your card, but I can't seem to find it. Do you have another?"

"Oh yeah, of course." He pulled one out of his wallet. He didn't give these out often, but now he was glad that he carried them around.

She looked down at it and smiled. "I've never had an artist for a friend before—" She snapped her mouth shut, regretting her use of the word *friend*. She hadn't meant to presume.

"Well, now you do."

CHAPTER 25

The homeless shelter's pastor offered to drop Stephen off at Walmart on his way to his meeting. Stephen had only spent one day with the man, and yet it was still weird to see him in a suit. Or maybe he was just feeling Galen's own discomfort. What kind of a pastor wouldn't be used to wearing a suit?

The one who runs a homeless shelter.

Stephen's phone buzzed in his pocket.

He didn't recognize the number, but it was from Maine, so he answered.

"Hi," Patrick said. "This kid is driving me nuts. Where are you?"

"Leaving here soon. I'll text you when I get to Jay."

"Hurry. He's refusing to sleep until he sees you, and he's so exhausted that he's staggering around the house like a drunk sailor."

Stephen laughed. "Sorry. Give him some chamomile tea."

Patrick lowered his voice. "He wants to go to Nana's house and go to sleep, but he's waiting for you. I don't even know if that's a good idea. I mean, what if he finds someone else?"

Oh boy. Was that a legitimate concern? "I think if there was anyone else there, one of us would have found them by now."

"I hope so."

"Anyway, I don't know if you want to let him join me. That's up to you, but that's exactly what I'm going to do. Everyone's acting like she won't be in that chair anymore. It's a nice idea, but I need to check."

Patrick didn't say anything.

"You've got some time to decide. I'll text you when I get to town, and then I'm going straight to bed." For once, that plan did not scare him.

"Okay. Text me, and we'll meet you at Nana's."

"Deal. Are you going to sit there and watch us sleep?"

He laughed. "Not sure, but I'm not leaving my son in that house without me, that's for sure." His protectiveness reminded Stephen of Carrie.

"How's your wife doing with all this?" She must think they'd all lost their minds.

"We told her everything. She believes us because she's a Jesus wacko. She feels bad because she says she was suspicious of you. Now she understands why you were acting so ... she used the word *peculiar*."

"She's forgiven."

"Good. She'll appreciate that. Okay, hurry home."

Stephen hung up, grateful that Jay, Maine was not his home anymore. He couldn't wait to get back to Nashville. He realized Galen was looking at him.

"If she's still in that chair, I'll eat my hat."

"How can you be so sure?"

Galen shook his head. "If she's still there, then none of this makes sense."

"None of this makes sense either way."

Galen smiled knowingly. "It will."

This annoyed Stephen. "What does that mean?"

"Sometimes we're slow to learn what God is trying to teach us. It wasn't a judgment. I'm the chief of slowpokes." He pulled his truck into the now crowded Walmart parking lot. "It's been a real pleasure to get to know you a little, Stephen. Please keep in touch."

He opened the door. "I will do that. Thank you for your help, really. We didn't have a backup plan."

Galen nodded. "Our church is usually the option *after* everyone has exhausted all their backup plans, so I'm honored you tried us first."

Stephen chuckled. The man had no idea how clueless they'd all been when they'd stumbled through his front doors.

The drive to Jay felt long. Stephen kept the window down and chomped on gum to help him stay awake. He was tempted to get some coffee, but he wanted to fall asleep the second he walked into Nana's house.

He pulled over in Livermore Falls to text Patrick that he was almost there.

"We're already here."

This news gave him a boost of energy that he sorely needed, and he completed his drive with some adrenaline flowing.

Sure enough, Patrick's car was in Nana's driveway.

Jeremiah ripped the door open and threw his small body into Stephen, who staggered back a step as he caught him.

"Thank God," Patrick said.

Stephen gently extricated himself from Jeremiah's embrace and stepped into the old house. He shut the door behind him. "For someone who's not into God, you sure do thank him a lot." He realized that might have sounded snarkier than he'd intended and added, "Not a criticism. Just an observation."

"Are you serious? After all this, I think it's safe to say that I'm a believer."

While this made sense, it still caught Stephen off guard, and he didn't know what to say.

"Isn't that good?" Jeremiah chirped. "He says he'll go to church with us tomorrow!" He turned toward the stairs. "I'm going to bed."

"Yeah, me too." He could hardly wait. His feet felt like fifty-pound weights as he trudged up the stairs. He kicked his shoes off, got under the covers, closed his eyes, and finally fell asleep.

CHAPTER 26

Stephen opened his eyes and looked at the walls, trying to figure out which world he was in. Slowly, he sat up, still unsure. But then he saw the door. It was different than the one he'd shut behind him before lying down, and it was now ajar.

He stood. "Jeremiah?" he called, realizing after his words split the silence that this was the first time he'd ever shouted in this world.

He heard footfall and went to the door.

"What took you so long?"

Stephen could feel fear and stepped closer to his young friend. "What's wrong?"

He shook his head. "Nothing."

A lie. "Jeremiah, what is it? Did you go there without me?"

Now he felt guilty.

"It's okay. I'm not mad, but what is it? Is she still there?" A horrible thought occurred to him then. Had she died? "Is she okay?"

He shook his head. "I didn't open the door." His voice grew quieter as he spoke.

"Okay, let's go take a look." Stephen started down the hallway, and Jeremiah didn't follow. Stephen stopped and looked back. "Jeremiah, just tell me. What is it?"

His eyes fell. "I heard a noise."

A scary noise.

"Tell me about it."

"It sounded like a monster, and it sounded really mad."

Stephen grew impatient. He was anxious to go look at that chair. "It'll be okay." He started walking, but still Jeremiah didn't move. This was quite the role reversal. "Do you want to stay here? Or go back to your room? I can go check the forepeak alone."

"Check the what?"

Stephen chuckled. "Her room. I can go check the chair."

Jeremiah shook his head. "Don't leave me."

Well, this stunk. Jeremiah was too scared to move and too scared to stay. But Stephen really needed to go check that chair.

"My dad plays video games."

Strange time to bring that up, but okay.

"And when he loses, sometimes he makes a loud mad noise and throws the controller."

"Okay."

"That's what the noise sounded like."

"Like your dad having a tantrum?"

He nodded. "But way bigger." He held his hands out to his sides to show the mass of the tantrum.

Stephen sighed. He didn't have the energy to deal with a tantrum-throwing monster. "Okay, well, you have the Holy Spirit in you, right? So the monster can't get you?" He felt guilty manipulating the boy, but he had to get moving.

Jeremiah nodded. "We should pray."

Irritation swelled in Stephen's chest. "Okay." He stepped closer. "Go ahead."

Jeremiah narrowed his eyes. "You have to pray too."

He did not want to do that.

"Not out loud. In your heart."

"Okay."

Jeremiah squeezed his eyes shut. "God, I am so scared. I think there's a monster in there. But you are bigger than all the monsters in the world. So protect us. Don't let it get us. Amen."

Stephen was deeply affected by this prayer, and he didn't like it. He tried to ignore the emotional reaction he was having, instead focusing on getting Jeremiah to the door.

But Jeremiah went willingly now, and they traveled down the long, dark hallway. Stephen strained to listen for sounds of otherworldly beings, but all he could hear were the floorboards protesting their weight, and their own breathing.

They reached the first floor's back hallway. Part of him wondered what was behind the other doors, but he forced himself to focus on the one up ahead on the left.

He paused with his door on the handle and listened. Then he gently pushed Jeremiah behind him.

"I don't hear it anymore," Jeremiah whispered. "I think it's gone." Stephen doubted that was true, and Jeremiah must have felt that doubt because he added, "If it's still here, God will protect us."

Stephen turned the knob and pushed.

The forepeak looked the same as it had looked the last time he'd been in it. He looked at the corner where shadows fled, but it was empty. He stepped into the room, and the metal floor moved beneath his feet. He'd been ready for it this time, but it was still disconcerting. This room was afloat. He didn't know how, but it was. He held his arms out for balance and hurried around the cargo—

The chair was empty. He let out a little cry of relief.

"She's gone!" Jeremiah cried.

"Yes, she is."

The ropes were still there. The lines she'd drawn in the dust—still there. But she was not there. "She's going to do it," Stephen said, mostly to himself. "She's going to get free."

"Let's go to the roof," Jeremiah said. His relief felt cool like menthol.

"Just a sec." Stephen pulled his phone out of his pocket and took a picture of the empty chair.

"Why'd you do that?"

"Just in case she ever has any doubts. Thought she might like to see the evidence."

"Good idea."

"Okay." He put his phone back into his pocket and gave that corner one more wary look. "Let's get out of here." They swiftly left that room and shut the door behind them. Stephen started toward the stairs.

"Wait!" Jeremiah said. "There's one more thing I have to do." He hurried away, expecting Stephen to stop him, and this told Stephen that he should try to do just that. Stephen strode his way but didn't reach him before he'd flung open the next door in the hallway. "It's empty!" he cried excitedly. He looked at Stephen. "I haven't explored all these rooms. We should check them, shouldn't we?"

His stomach sank. If they found someone else, he thought it might break him. "Yes, we should."

Jeremiah ran to the next one. It was a bare room with wooden walls and a wooden floor. A thick layer of undisturbed dust covered the floor. Not so much as a spider's footprint.

"Okay. Next one." One by one, they opened each door in that very long hallway, but they found no one else bound and gagged. They found no evidence that anyone else had ever been in this part of the house, in these extra rooms.

They finished their check and then faced each other in the dark back hallway.

"Roof?" Jeremiah asked, his voice tinged with hope.

"Nope. Bed."

Jeremiah sighed. "Fine."

Stephen followed him up the stairs. He could feel what the boy was feeling, and their emotions were a perfect match. That never happened. But it was happening now. Both were at peace. And both were satisfied with having finished the job and done it well.

CHAPTER 27

His Mansion didn't let their residents have cell phones, so Stephen had to call the front desk. The woman who answered was polite, but she wouldn't let him speak to Rosie. She did, however, offer to relay a message to her, and he scrambled to think of one that would convey everything important. "Can you tell her that the chair is empty?" Turned out the message wasn't so complicated after all.

"The chair is empty?" the woman repeated.

"Yes, please. It's important. Also, can you ask her to call me when she can?"

"Yes, of course. What's your number?"

"She has it," he said, suddenly in a hurry to get off the phone. He hoped she still had his number. He thanked the woman and hung up.

Rosie didn't call until a full week later. Stephen was back in Nashville, back in the fast-paced swing of things and in a meeting when his caller ID read "New Hampshire."

"I'm so sorry," he said, standing up and heading for the door. "I have to take this." His exit surprised everyone. Most of the people in the room knew he didn't have anyone in his personal life that he would leave a meeting for.

Of course, no one knew about Rosie.

"Hello?" He ducked into a stairwell and then regretted it because the reception was awful in the concrete tower. "Hang on." He scaled the steps to the next floor, escaped the stairwell, and headed for a window. "Hey, Rosie. How are you feeling?"

"I have good moments and not so good ones, but they're mostly good."

"That's great to hear."

"Thank you so much for your message. They thought you were nuts, but I assured them that it made perfect sense. Tried to assure them, anyway." She sounded so different. Familiar, but new.

"You didn't tell them what it meant?" He really hoped not.

"Oh no," she said quickly. "I've learned that not all Christians are as ready to believe crazy stories as Pastor Galen was."

Stephen chuckled, suddenly missing that guy.

"But it was a big help. It was a relief, but it gave me a lot of hope. Like, I'm really going to do it this time."

"Yes, I think that you are."

The line went quiet.

"So I asked you to call me back because I took a picture. I was thinking I could send you a copy."

"Oh, you're so awesome. I would *love* to have a copy."

"I thought maybe. I knew you weren't allowed to have a phone, but can I email it to you?"

"Yeah sure."

"Great. Do you still have my card? My email address was on it. If you shoot me an email, I'll reply with the photo."

"Yes, I have your card. I will email you as soon as I get off the phone."

"Great."

"Great."

The line fell quiet again.

"Stephen, I don't know how to thank you ... I'm struggling right now, but I am so, so much better than I was a week ago. I wish you could see me, so you'd know that."

"I believe you," he said quickly. "And I'll tell Jeremiah too."

"I already wrote him a letter." She laughed. "Figured his parents might not want him talking on the phone with me."

"Ah, I think this whole thing might have loosened them up some."

"How about you?"

"Me? I'm good."

"That's good to hear, but I meant has the whole thing loosened you up?"

"Uh ... I think I was pretty loose to begin with."

She hesitated. "I'm trying to ask about God."

"Oh." Ugh. Did he really need to do this? "Maybe we can talk about that later."

She laughed lightly. "Okay. But I am telling you that beyond a shadow of a doubt, he is real. He is real, and he loves you. I have *felt* him. I have felt his love. And I want you to feel it too, so I'm praying for you every day."

How did she know what he thought about God? And shouldn't he be the one praying for her? A pang of guilt stabbed him. It hadn't even occurred to him to do that. Maybe he should find a church and figure out how to pray for her.

She laughed again. "Well, I'll let you go. I'm sure you're at work. But I wanted to thank you. I'll email you right away, but no hurry on getting back to me."

"Okay."

"But don't forget."

"I won't. I promise. Rosie?"

"Yeah?"

"You take good care, okay?"

"I will. You too."

By the time he got back to his meeting, she had already emailed. He sent her the photo and then tried to get his mind back on his work, but when the meeting was over, he had no idea what they'd discussed.

CHAPTER 28

Stephen sat in his rental car, waiting for Patrick and Jeremiah to arrive. While he was incredibly grateful for His Mansion and had learned that the facility's methods worked, he was still weirded out by the place. Though he'd talked to Rosie several times in the last few months, and though she'd avidly preached Jesus in each of those conversations, six months back home in Nashville had tempered the effects of his supernatural experiences. Sometimes he could even pretend the whole week had never happened. He was used to being normal again, so all of these Jesus freaks in one place? Not his cup of tea.

And he knew they were Jesus freaks. He'd visited Rosie once, two months after she'd checked in. She'd looked better, it had been awkward, and they hadn't had much to talk about. They had brainwashed her completely. She was entirely smitten with Jesus.

Stephen didn't wish that away for her, because it was working. She was sober. She was happy. She was taking classes and building a future. But that didn't mean he wanted it for himself. Yet since that visit, her pleas had only intensified. She was genuinely worried about where he was going to spend eternity.

It occurred to him that she'd traded one addiction for another: heroin for Jesus. He didn't fully believe that, but if it were true, her new addiction was a whole lot safer.

And she was happy. Still, he didn't want to face her without the buffer that Patrick and Jeremiah would provide.

But before they got there, Galen and Maggie pulled into the parking lot and spotted him. They smiled brightly and headed his way.

Grudgingly, he got out of the car.

Galen tapped on the hood. "Is this yours?"

"No, it's a rental."

"Oh good." He looked relieved.

"What?" Stephen asked.

"I've heard these are nothing but trouble. Glad you didn't pay forty thousand dollars for it."

Maggie rolled her eyes. "He used to be a mechanic." She hugged his arm and leaned into him like a teenager on a date.

"Still am when I have the time."

"Which is never."

"Anyway, let's go in," Galen said.

Stephen fell into step alongside them.

"Have you seen her since she's been here?" Galen asked.

"Only once. She looked great."

"Yeah, Maggie's talked to her. Sounds like quite a miracle." Galen slapped him on the back. "And it all started with you." He grinned. "Nice work."

Stephen chuckled uncomfortably. It all felt so far away now. So impossible. *Like dreams do.*

Just before they got to the door, Galen stopped and looked at him. "Can I be nosy?"

"Sure."

"Have you had any other ... have you seen anything else in the spiritual realm?"

"The spiritual realm?" That was a new one.

Galen nodded. "Yeah."

"Uh, no. Not even close. It's been a wonderfully ordinary six months." This news surprised and disappointed the pastor. Stephen hadn't realized he'd been so invested.

"That's interesting," Galen said.

"Come on, honey." Maggie tugged on his arm.

"Just a sec. Stephen, you know, not many people get to do what you did. What you and Jeremiah did. You might have a gift."

"I don't know if I'd call it that."

More people were coming, and Galen led them to the side of the path to get out of the way.

Maggie sighed in annoyance.

"What would you call it, then?"

"I don't know. I called it having bad dreams when I visited my Nana. Then I called it the craziest week of my life. And now it's over."

Galen studied him. "But you saved her life."

He didn't know what to say to that.

"There could be other people to help," Galen said quietly.

Stephen tried to laugh that suggestion off. "I've lived in several other buildings including the house I grew up in and a college dorm, and I've never had dreams like that anywhere else. It wasn't me that was special. It was that house." As he spoke the words, he doubted them.

"Okay. And how many other people slept in that house over the years?"

Stephen knew where he was going with that. "Point taken. Then it was the combination. But I'm telling you, there's nothing special about me apart from that house."

"Interesting."

That word was starting to annoy Stephen.

"Did you know that Jeremiah and his folks have visited our church a few times?"

Oh boy.

"And I've had some good talks with them. Jeremiah tells me that he has a pretty significant ability. I don't know what to call it. Strong intuition or a sixth sense? Something like that. He can feel what other people are feeling. He says you can do that too."

"I've always called it empathy." Stephen was desperate to play this down.

Galen nodded. "Yeah. Empathy. That's a good word for it. But lots of people have empathy."

Maggie was tugging again.

"Sorry, I'm not trying to pressure you." He meant it. He held both hands up. "It's good to see you, so I'm excited to talk to you. Sorry if I come on too strong." He took a step back. "But I spend my life trying to help people, and I sure wish I had an ounce of what you have."

"It's not always a good thing."

Galen laughed. "Oh I'm sure it doesn't always feel good. But spinach doesn't feel good either, and yet it's good. Anyway, I'll leave you alone. But if you ever want to talk about it, I'm all ears. And if not, I understand. Just be open to what God has for you? Please? Keep your eyes open. You never know what God might let you see." He smiled again and then turned and headed for the door.

Stephen froze. Galen's words had opened a door in his head, and the thoughts and feelings rushing to and fro through that doorway were making him woozy.

Keep your eyes open. You never know what God might let you see.

That sounded a lot like Nana's final plea: *Let God show you what he wants you to see.*

He didn't know much, but he knew beyond the shadow of a doubt that this was not a coincidence.

And this realization made him angry. Why? Why did he have to be wrestling with this? He'd come here to support Rosie, not to have a spiritual awakening, not to suffer a religious conversion.

He closed his eyes and tried to get a grip. *Just get through this service and then get your butt home, and you can forget all about all of this—again.* Stephen liked his life the way it was. He was happy. He'd worked hard to get where he was. If God had more to show him, and if it resembled what God had let him see so far, he wanted *nothing* to do with it.

CHAPTER 29

As Stephen's eyes adjusted to the dim indoor light, he hardly recognized the woman sprinting down the aisle toward them. For starters, she was squealing. Once he'd realized it was Rosie, he'd thought she was going for Maggie, but she breezed right past her friend and leapt at him.

He almost didn't catch her, but he managed to get his arms around her in time.

His arms had as much trouble recognizing her as his eyes had. She was stronger, thicker—she was more alive.

Her feet returned to the floor, and she pulled back. "Welcome," she said, and there was a light in her eyes that had definitely not been there the first time they'd met. She gave the same hug, minus the running start, to Maggie and then a third hug to Galen. Then she turned back to Stephen. "Come on!" She took his hand into hers. "They gave each of us a family section, and you're my family." She led them to the front row and pointed to some empty chairs. "Thank you so much for coming. I know it's far for all of you." She squeezed Stephen's hand. "Especially you." Then she let go of him, and they all sat down.

She stood in front of them, subtly swinging back and forth, making her skirt swish around her knees.

"Is your mother coming?" Maggie asked.

"No. I invited her, but no." Rosie was only a little sad about this.

"Why are you nervous?" Stephen asked and then immediately wished he hadn't. He'd asked because he was genuinely concerned, but he hadn't meant to accuse her of being nervous or to tell everyone else that she was.

"I'm giving a little speech."

"Really?" Maggie said. "They make you do that?"

"No, they don't make us. But they strongly encourage it. And it's okay. I wanted to." She looked at Stephen. "I've learned so much that I'm eager to share. But you're right. I am nervous. There are a lot of people here. I guess some people have more family than I do."

"Quality over quantity," Stephen joked.

"Yes, and here comes my favorite now." She took off running again, and Stephen turned in his chair to see that Jeremiah had arrived. He'd grown about three inches, and he ran too, meeting her in the aisle. They embraced, and then she led him and his parents to the rest of them.

Maggie and Galen enjoyed a little reunion with Jeremiah's parents, which made Stephen feel left out. He smiled at Jeremiah. "How's it going? How was the drive?"

"Good." He settled in beside Stephen. "Isn't this cool?"

"Yeah. It is."

Jeremiah smiled at him. "We really did it."

Stephen was tired of being given credit. He didn't say anything.

"I miss it. Our adventures. My life is so boring now."

Someday Jeremiah would understand that boring was a good goal.

The band started playing, and Rosie went up onto the stage and stood in front of a short row of chairs. The band sang two churchy songs and then left the stage, and the executive director welcomed everybody to the service and prayed. Then he introduced one of the counselors, who gave a short speech about how hard these three graduates had worked to get to where they were today. And then he introduced the first graduate, Rosie McAllister.

Rosie stepped up to the podium and took a deep breath. "Hi everyone. I'm Rosie. Thank you for coming."

And in that second, Stephen knew that Rosie was doing a better job at life than he was.

"When they first invited us to share our personal testimony, I nearly died from fright. But then I figured public speaking couldn't be much harder than kicking heroin, right?"

A polite laugh rippled through the room.

She cleared her throat and looked down at her note cards. She read from them, sharing her story, leaving out the supernatural parts and starting with running from the cops and finding herself at Open Door Church. As she spoke, she grew more confident, and Stephen relaxed with the absence of her stage fright.

"I remember the first time I tried drugs. I remember how good it felt, and how I thought, I always want to feel like this. But I also remember who I was back then. I remember the path I was on.

"I was the girl in high school that everyone told their problems to. I was such a good listener. I was good at keeping secrets. I was pretty good at giving advice. Well, at least I thought I was." She laughed. "And I remember thinking that I wanted to be a school counselor. Our school didn't have one. Well, we did, but we had to share her with like five other schools, so she was never really around. And so I thought that would be a good job for me. Of course, that all went away. I didn't go to college. I barely graduated from high school. But when I decided to get clean, Pastor Galen said something to me. He said it more than once, and I'm so grateful because the first time he said it, I didn't believe him. In fact, I thought he was nuts. It seemed so unlikely. But over these last few months, as God has become realer and realer to me, as I literally heard his voice and felt his arms around me, holding me while I shook with fear and grief and shame, I became more and more sure of those words. Here's what Galen said. 'God has big plans for you.' So simple, right? It's probably true of everyone. But when it's you that's receiving that message, it's pretty powerful, right?

"I thought I was already dead. I was in a prison cell. I thought that the drugs would keep me happy and high, but that's not how it works because so much bad stuff happens while you're trying to stay happy and high. So anyway, I had totally given up. So for me to realize that there was still a plan? Well, that kept me going. I wanted to know what that plan was. I wanted to get in on that plan, to do what I was supposed to do, to do what I was meant to do. I have wasted so much time. And so I've been taking classes, and I'm on track to earn my BA in psychology with a focus on addictions through Southern New Hampshire University."

The room erupted with applause, and Stephen had never been so proud of anyone. He exchanged a look with Jeremiah, who was feeling the same.

"Thank you for the applause, but this really isn't about me, and I need to finish up anyway, as there are two other graduates."

Several people laughed. This crowd loved her. She was a star. It was so cool to see the real Rosie.

"What I'm trying to say is that I know there are other people in this room who don't know that there are plans for them. Super fun, awesome, inspiring plans. Please, I'm begging you, don't waste time like I did." She looked Stephen in the eye. "There's a plan. And I think if you look back over your life, and if you're honest, you'll see evidence of that plan already." She turned her eyes back to the center of the room and flashed them another dazzling smile. "Thank you, and God bless you."

CHAPTER 30

S tephen stood alone outside with his face upturned and his eyes closed, enjoying the feel of the sunlight on his face.

"How are you doing?"

He opened his eyes to see Maggie smiling at him. "I'm okay."

"Good. That was some speech she gave, wasn't it?"

He laughed. "Yeah. She's really something."

"I had a feeling that she had a specific audience in mind."

He groaned. "Yeah, and she didn't really need to do that. She's already given me similar speeches in private."

Maggie laughed. "Good for her. Maybe she thought it would mean more coming from a stage."

If so, she'd been right. It had meant more.

"So are you convinced yet? Do you believe God has plans for you?"

"What about you? Did you always know you were going to be a pastor's wife?"

She laughed. "Nice deflection. And hardly! I thought I was going to marry the rich lawyer I was living with. But, like she said, God had other plans."

She'd been shacked up with her boyfriend? Wasn't that a giant no-no with these people? "Have you always been a Christian?"

"No, not even close. I didn't even hear the gospel till I was an adult."

The gospel. The old story. He'd heard it a hundred times. "And when you heard it, what made you think it was ... real?"

Her smile fell away, and her eyes grew serious. "Do you think it's real?"

"I don't know," he admitted. "I have trouble believing that it is. It's just all so absurd."

"Stephen, how can you see what you've seen and not believe?"

He shook his head. "I don't know."

She stared at him. "But you can feel what others are feeling, right? I've heard about your grandmother. She was a warrior. Couldn't you feel her faith?"

He nodded. "I could. But I'm also an educated man, a man of reason. I can't believe in things that don't make sense."

"Oh! Is that the problem? Well, have you heard about the sand dunes in California that sing?"

He uttered a short, shocked laugh. "What?"

"Yep. Look it up. Sand mountains. Singing. Okay, that's not a good example because you've never heard of it. How about the seals?"

"What about them?"

"You know that seals can return to the exact spot they were born, and that's where they breed?"

"Yeah, I've heard that." Where was she going with this?

"And you believe it?"

He shrugged. "Sure."

"But can you explain it?"

"What? No. I'm not a zoologist.

"Okay, but you understand it, right? It makes sense to you?"

"No." He was annoyed. This beautiful saintly pastor's wife was downright annoying.

"But you believe that it's true."

"Why would anyone make up a story about breeding seals?"

"Why would anyone make up a story about a poor carpenter coming back to life?"

"To control people," he said quickly. "To manipulate people. For money. For power."

"Religion did that, not Jesus. And the new way of living that Jesus taught doesn't do that either." She squared her body to his, and he nearly shrank back. "Those first disciples? Those first followers of Jesus? Think about it. There were twelve apostles. Eleven were brutally murdered. One was banished to an island for convicts, and the only reason they banished him was because they tried to boil him alive and he survived, so they were scared he couldn't die. And you know what? They all stuck to their story. All twelve of them. They never wavered no matter how much pain they were in or how scared they got. I don't think any of them would have suffered and died for a lie, let alone all of them."

He was fresh out of arguments. "Maybe you should be the preacher."

She laughed. "I don't think that's in God's plan for me, but you can feel my faith right now?"

"I can." It felt like heat on his skin. It was unpleasant and uncomfortable.

"Good. Feel my sincerity when I say that the things I've seen ... they can't be explained by reason. But I saw them. They were real. They involved people I know and love and trust. It wasn't tricks and special effects, just like it wasn't tricks and special effects when you woke up in a room that didn't exist and found a girl tied to a chair."

His doubts were weakening, and that wasn't a pleasant feeling either.

"Do me a favor, and I'll leave you alone."

He chuckled. "Depends on the favor."

CHAPTER 31

Maggie smiled brightly. "All I want you to do is read three verses. Really read them, though, okay? Think about them for a bit. Your life depends on it."

Stephen nodded, though he doubted very much that his life depended on ancient scriptures. "Three verses?"

"Three verses."

"Which three?" Were there three freakishly long verses in the Bible?

"First chapter in Romans. Reading the whole first chapter would be awesome—" Great, the favor was already growing. "—but at least read 18, 19, and 20."

He nodded. "I can do that." A small price to pay to end this uncomfortable situation.

"Thank you. You have the truth of those three verses, you have your own doubts, and you have what you've seen with your own two eyes. I don't think those three things can coexist. One of them has to go."

And he knew exactly which one she wanted to get rid of.

She gave him a tight hug that lasted longer than he expected. Then she let go and stepped back. "I think the absolute world of you, Stephen. I am so excited to see what God's going to do."

He watched her walk away and then waited for Rosie to come outside.

Jeremiah and his parents came first. "Hey, did you hear that we got an offer on Nana's house?" Patrick said.

Stephen nodded. He had heard that, though it was their parents who had gotten the offer, not the grandkids, but he didn't bother to correct him. "I did hear that. Good news."

"Kind of weird to think about, though, right?"

Stephen shook his head. He'd given this plenty of thought. "I don't think so. Will those rooms exist if Jeremiah and I aren't there to visit them? I don't know, but they might not."

"Okay, let's talk about something else," Carrie said.

Patrick rolled his eyes. "She's still not comfortable with the whole thing. Just one more thing, honey, before he runs back to Nashville."

Stephen ground his back teeth together. He wasn't *running* anywhere.

"I don't think that's the case," Patrick said. "I've been really digging into the Bible, and I think there's a lot of stuff going on ..." He waved his hands over his head, looking like a complete lunatic. "Things that we can't see. I think those rooms are still there, but most of us can't see them."

Stephen shrugged. "Well I don't think they can do much harm if no one is trapped in them. Right?"

"Amen, brother. Amen."

Stephen cringed. Patrick had crossed over. He completely belonged to the other side now. They all did.

Finally, Rosie came outside and made a beeline for them. Patrick, Carrie, and Jeremiah said their congratulations and goodbyes, and then Carrie tried to usher them toward the parking lot, leaving Stephen alone with Rosie for the first time.

"Nice speech."

She smiled brightly. "I'm glad you liked it."

"You never told me that you wanted to be a counselor when you were young."

She sighed. "Yeah. It's kind of scary to share my dream because sometimes it seems so unrealistic."

"You were in high school when you first went to Nana's house."

"I was."

"And you were Patrick's age."

"Yup." She was curious where he was going with this.

"Do you remember what time of year it was when you visited Nana's house?"

She hesitated, studying him. "I don't think so, why?"

"It doesn't matter, but I was just thinking ..." He almost didn't finish his question, but he didn't want it to gnaw at him for years to come. "When I was fourteen I vowed to never sleep in my Nana's house again. I was sick of having the dreams, and I'd gotten busy with high school, so while I visited her still, I didn't spend the night again. And it seems like that was right around the time that you visited for the first time. So I'm just ..."

"You're hoping you weren't dreaming in that house when I was first trapped there?"

He nodded, his throat getting tight. "To think I could have helped you way back then."

She stared off into the distance. "I don't know, but I don't think it matters."

"It matters to me."

She looked at him and smiled. "Please don't let it. If there was any overlap, it's okay. It's all worked out."

"But you've suffered so much ..." He wiped at his eyes. "Okay, sorry. I guess if we don't know, we don't know, and I guess that has to be okay."

"It is okay, Stephen. I promise. So your flight leaves tonight?"

He nodded, grateful for the redirection. "Yeah, I've got to get back. Things are really busy at work right now." People might assume there wasn't a sense of urgency in the art world, but that wasn't true in Nashville.

"I understand. But you'll come visit me? See my new apartment?"

"Absolutely. And you're welcome in Nashville anytime."

"Yeah, I guess that would be a more exciting destination, right?" She laughed. "Will you take me to the Grand Ole Opry?"

"Sure. And then I'll show you a hundred other awesome things that the city has to offer."

"Sounds like a date. Okay then." She gave him another hug, squeezed him tightly, and then stepped back. "I'm not giving up on you. I'm praying for you every day till you tell me that you believe."

Between Nana and Rosie, Stephen had not lived very many days without someone praying for him. "I guess there's no point in arguing with you."

"There is not. Thank you for coming today. I know you're busy."

"You're welcome. And I'm really glad I came. You're an inspiration."

She pointed at the sky. "All the credit goes to him."

Yeah, yeah. "See you around." He turned and headed back to his rental, excited to get home and back to the real world.

CHAPTER 32

S tephen sat in the airport, waiting for his delayed plane to show up. He was scrolling through social media and getting annoyed when he remembered Maggie's request. The first chapter of Romans. Three verses.

He looked them up on his phone:

For the wrath of God ...

Oh sure, start me off with some brimstone, why don't you?

... is revealed from heaven against all ungodliness and unrighteousness of men ...

This is scary stuff. Pastor's wife gets aggressive.

... who hinder the truth in unrighteousness.

Wait. What? God reveals his wrath against sin. Okay, that makes sense. But he reveals his wrath on those who hinder the truth? Those are fighting words. I don't even know what truth is. And suddenly, he was very, very nervous about hindering it.

He reread that verse again and then went on to the next:

Because that which is known of God is manifest in them; for God manifested it unto them.

This was too complicated. He grew annoyed. But he'd promised her three verses, and he'd only read two. Plus, he felt challenged to prove her wrong. These words, his reason, and his experiences could all coexist perfectly well, thank you very much.

But what did this verse mean? He knew what each of the words meant, but what did they mean together? Wasn't it a bit redundant? These men knew about God because God had shown them what they were supposed to know? Wasn't that circular reasoning?

His breath caught, and he sat up straighter. *Oh no.* God had shown him so much. God had shown him *God.*

He almost couldn't bear to keep reading, but he had to know the rest.

For the invisible things of him since the creation of the world are clearly seen, being perceived through the things that are made, even his everlasting power and divinity; that they may be without excuse.

Stephen felt sick.

He had no excuse.

He'd seen so much in his life. Before even counting the supernatural stuff that no one else was privileged enough to see, he had seen so much beauty in this world.

He had no excuse.

He turned his phone screen to black and closed his eyes. He needed a break.

But now there was a gnawing hunger in his gut—a hunger for knowledge. A hunger to understand. He opened his eyes and read the verses again. And again. And then he remembered that there were other translations of the ancient Greek, and he looked those up.

And after reading several different translations, the truth was so clear that he started to cry.

He'd been wrong.

The truth was: Evil tries to suppress, erase, squelch truth. God sends his wrath on this evil and on the people who spread it. They have no excuse, no defense of their evil because God has made the truth plain to them. They should know this truth, and they would if they would just allow themselves to see it.

He'd been so, so wrong.

So, so arrogant.

"I'm sorry, God," he whispered.

He thought about these verses and about what it meant for his life until they called him for boarding. When they told him to put his devices on airplane mode, he shot off a quick email to Maggie: "I get it now."

The plane took off, and he watched New England shrink into nothingness. Nana had told him to let God show him what God wanted him to see. The pastor had told him to keep his eyes open.

What if he'd had his eyes open when he was fourteen? Maybe he could have saved Rosie then. And what if there were other people like her out there now, suffering? What if he could help them if he would only open his eyes?

He didn't think he was ready for that. He didn't want to commit to that. But neither could he convince himself any longer that God wasn't very real and very active in this world. Now that he had accepted the truth, he was accountable to it, and that made him very, very uncomfortable.

Let God show you what he wants you to see.

But what if he didn't want to see it?

Too bad.

It wasn't about him.

He closed his eyes and prayed, *Okay. I give up. You've shown me the truth over and over, and I've tried not to see it. I'm sorry. Please show me what you want me to see. I don't know if I'm ready, but I'm willing.*

Then Stephen opened his eyes. And he saw.

Made in the USA
Las Vegas, NV
02 February 2023

66739075R00111